The BRUBACK LIBRARY

JOEY PIGZA LOSES CONTROL

JACK GANTOS

Joey Pigza Loses Control

SCHOLASTIC INC.
New York Toronto London Auckland Sydney
Mexico City New Delhi Hong Kong Buenos Aires

ISBN 0-439-33898-0

Published by Scholastic Inc., 555 Broadway, New York, NY 10012,
by arrangement with Farrar, Straus and Giroux.

12 11 10 9 8 7 6 5 6

Printed in the U.S.A. 23

First Scholastic printing, September 2001

Designed by Judy Lanfredi

For Anne and Mabel

JOEY PIGZA LOSES CONTROL

1

POTHOLES

We were on our way to Dad's house and Mom was driving with both hands clamped tightly around the wheel as if she had me by the neck. I had been snapping my seat belt on and off and driving her nuts by asking a hundred *what if*'s about Dad. She'd been hearing them for two weeks already and wasn't answering. But that didn't stop me. What if he's not nice? What if he hates me? What if he's as crazy as you always said he was? What if he drinks and gets nasty? What if I don't like him? What if Grandma tries to put me in the refrigerator again? What if they make Pablo sleep outside? What if they don't eat pizza? What if I want to come home quick, can I hire a helicopter?

"Yes," she said to my last question, not really listening. She was taking the long roller-coaster way to

Pittsburgh, which was up and down about a million mountain backroads, because she was afraid of driving too fast on the turnpike. As she said before we loaded up the borrowed car, "My license is slightly expired and I don't have insurance, so just bear with me."

"How can something be slightly expired?" I asked. "Is that the same as day-old bread? What if we get stopped by the police? What if we are arrested? What if the jails for boys and dogs look like giant birdcages?" She didn't answer me then, and she wasn't answering my questions now, even though I kept asking. All she did was tighten her grip and lean forward so much her chin was touching the top of the steering wheel. After a while her silence beat my talking like paper covers rock, so I kept my mouth shut even though the list of questions kept sprouting in my brain.

But then Pablo, my Chihuahua, started yapping nonstop. Maybe it was his neck she was thinking of squeezing because he was driving her nuts too. The roads were beat up and I asked her not to hit the holes because Pablo has a weak stomach and gets carsick easily, but she didn't even try to steer around the bumps and holes. Her elbows were shaking and her jaw was so tight her front teeth were denting her lower lip. I knew she was stressed-out with the thought of seeing Dad, but right now I was more concerned about Pablo.

"Go around the holes!" I kept shouting as I rubbed Pablo's swollen belly with the very tippity tips of my fingertips. He was lying on his back with his four feet up in the air like he was already dead, except his eyes were twitching.

"When you're driving you can't exactly zigzag down the road!" she hollered back. "We could lose control and flip over."

"Well, Pablo's stomach is about to flip," I said, warning her.

"Then hold your hand over his snout," she suggested, and squeezed the steering wheel a little tighter as the car stumbled along.

"Then he'll get carsick through his ears," I replied. "Or worse, it will back up and shoot out his you-know-where."

She glanced over at me and glared. "You better keep his you-know-where aimed out the window," she ordered. "I don't want any nasty accidents."

Just then we hit a deep hole and I lifted up off my seat. I saw another one coming and I took my hand from Pablo's fizzing snout and reached for the steering wheel and Mom slapped my hand away just as the tire hit the hole hard and I bounced sideways and cracked my head on the half-open window and Pablo flipped over onto his hind legs like he was doing a wheelie then opened his mouth and did what I said he'd do all over the front of the radio.

"Oh, sugar!" Mom spit out. "Sugar, sugar, sugar!"

I knew that word meant trouble. The last time she said "sugar" like that was when she got the letter from Dad's lawyer in the mail and I knew it wasn't because she had something sweet in her mouth.

"Open the glove box," Mom said. "There might be some napkins in there."

I pressed the lock and the little door dropped down and smacked Pablo on his bandaged ear, which must have hurt. There was a box of tissues inside so I pulled that out and because I didn't know what to do with Pablo I tucked him into the glove box and snapped the door shut. He started yapping again and I pressed my lips to the thin seam around the door and whispered, "Go to sleep. I'll wake you when we get there." He whimpered for a moment, then settled down. I tugged out a wad of tissues and began to clean the mess out from between all the little knobs and buttons on the radio, which was hard to do because the car was jerking around in all directions, so I quit.

I let Mom settle down for a mile or two while I chewed on my fingernails before she caught me and pulled my hand from my mouth and held it tight.

"Do you want me to drive?" I asked.

"I guess you may have noticed I'm a nervous wreck?" she started. "Well, I just can't get my mind off your dad."

That's one thing I liked about him already. Her mind was on *him*, *him*, *him*. Usually it was on *me*, *me*, *me*, and I couldn't do or say anything that she didn't notice, but now I was hiding inside his shadow like a drop inside an ocean, and he got to take the blame for her bad nerves.

"You know I have mixed feelings about letting you do this," she said. She was starting to get weepy so it was my turn to settle her down.

"What if he's nice?" I guessed.

"He better be nice," she replied.

"I mean really nice?" I said. "Like when you first met him."

"He wasn't even nice then. He was just okay."

"Well, did you kiss him on the lips?"

"What do you think?" she said.

Just the thought of her kissing Dad made me silly and I began to sing, "Mom and Dad sitting in a tree k-i-s-s-i-n-g."

"Stop that!" she snapped. "You're buggin' me again."

I took a breather then started up again. "Have I done something wrong?" I asked.

"No," she replied. "I just have a case of bad nerves."

"Then, why are you sending me to Dad if you don't think he's any good?"

"I'm not sending you because *I* like him," she replied. "I'm sending you because *you* might like him and because I think—not with my heart—that it is a good thing for you to have a relationship with your father. And now that he claims to have stopped drinking and has a job and has gone to court to get some visitation, I'm sending you to him because I think it's the right thing to do. But don't ask me how I *feel* about all this."

"How do you *feeeeel*?" I asked, and leaned forward and pressed my smiley face into her shoulder.

"Don't go there," she said. "I really don't want to feel anything about all this."

"Mom and Dad, sitting in a tree, k-i-s-s-i-n-g!" I sang again with my head bouncing as if my neck was a big spring.

"Now, Joey," Mom said, lifting one hand off the steering wheel and pushing me back to my side. "Get serious. Don't cling to the notion that me and him are going to get back together. No way is that going to happen, so just let it go and focus on your relationship with your father. You have six weeks with him. Figure out what *you* want from this guy before you get there. Give it some thought because he can be, you know, wired like you, only he's *bigger*."

Even as she talked I didn't listen because I liked what I was thinking more than what she was telling me so I just hummed, "Mom and Dad, sitting in a tree . . ."

After that she re-gripped the steering wheel and seemed to aim for the holes. Some quiet time passed and since she didn't pay any attention to me I said, "Are you sending me because of my trouble with Pablo?"

"That's only part of it," she said. "But that last little *business* was a wake-up call for me—and for Pablo. I mean, I can't keep you locked up in the house all summer."

The little *business* she referred to made me hang my head, because it was all my fault, and like most everything wrong I did, she felt responsible so I just slumped into the corner of my seat. I put my tiny tape-player speakers in my ears and turned on the music. Herb Alpert and the Tijuana Brass were playing "Lollipops and Roses" and while I nodded along I added up the good and bad things about my behavior that day, which is what my special-ed teacher told me to do when I felt sad.

Before I had gone to special ed and got my new meds it would have been impossible for me to sit still and make a list of good and bad things. I didn't have time for lists. I didn't have time for anything that lasted longer than the snap of my fingers. But after I got my good meds, which were in a patch I stuck on my body every day, I started to settle down and think. And not just think about all the bad things that had already happened. I started thinking about the good things I wanted to happen. And the best part about thinking good things was that now I could make them come true instead of having everything I wanted blow up in my face.

So, as I sat in the car and took a deep breath, I asked myself what I wanted from Dad. Even though I thought for a long time, my list was short. There was really only one thing I wanted. So after a while I sat up and told Mom.

"I just want him to love me as much as I already love him," I said.

She listened, then pursed her lips before saying, "Honey, I'm sure he does." Her voice sounded like she had a long list of other things to say, but didn't.

2

DOG-EARED

Bad things started not long after school had ended and Mom was leaving me home alone all day because she had to work. She had given me a trumpet and the Herb Alpert tape and wanted me to learn all the songs, but it was too hard so I only learned a few of the sounds. Mostly, Pablo and I hung out in our fenced-in little back yard, which was all dirt and rocks and dry islands of dead grass that looked like knotted-up troll hairs and were as hard to pull up as if I was pulling one of those wrinkly little people right out of the ground. Pablo and I were digging into the dirt with the splintered handle of a broken baseball bat and collecting good throwing rocks. When I got a pile of them, about twenty-five roundish ones, I started throwing them like some maniac pitching machine—*wham! wham! wham!*—one right after another at a target I had drawn on the wood fence and their echo cracked through the neighborhood. I was so good I almost got a bull's-eye every time. But then I got bored and had to make it harder so I bent over and sidearmed one between my legs. I wasn't so good that way because the stone went flying over the fence and then I heard something break so I stopped and ran inside. A few minutes later a man knocked on our door but I was hiding behind the couch and after he said some bad words he finally went away.

That's when I searched the house for new things to do and found the dart set in the attic. There was a lot of game stuff up there that must have belonged to my dad and since he wasn't in the picture anymore I took it for mine. I went down to the living room and drew a bunch of animals with bull's-eye heads on pieces of paper which I taped on couch pillows. I scattered them around the room then started to practice. I'd spin around a few times then screech to a sudden stop and wing a dart at the closest bull's-eye. I was pretty good and really liked having to throw the darts when I was dizzy. Even as the room was spinning like a wobbly carousel I was pretty good. I hit all my targets, somewhere. And one time I kept spinning until everything was blurry like when you tape bottle bottoms over your eyes and when I stopped I threw a dart at the first animal I saw and heard Pablo yelp and when I could get my balance back and focus my eyes I found him quivering in a corner of the couch with a dart through his ear. I called to him but he didn't say a word. At first he just sat there stunned and stared with his shiny bug-eyes at me like he couldn't believe I had hurt him and then he went nuts and was running around the room yapping and hopping and dragging that dart around. When I finally cornered him I told him he was going to be okay. And he was okay, because the dart had just gone through the skin and made a clean hole. It was like I had poked it through a soft piece of suede. There was only about a drop of blood spilled, but the sight of blood really makes him hysterical. So I held him down and tried to cover his eyes as I pulled the dart out. He went berserk, and I got worried the hole might get infected and he would have to have his ear amputated and go to his own doggy special-ed for disabled dogs, so I wrapped him up and carried him down to the hair salon to get Mom's opinion on if we should take Pablo to the vet or just put one of my old patches on him. She was in the middle of teasing out a woman's hair when I brought Pablo in wrapped in a bath towel, and she gave me a pretty stressed-out look. "It was an accident that the dart went through his ear," I explained. "I was aiming at a moose."

"Aw, sugar!" she said. "Sugar! Sugar! Now let me see what you've done to poor Pablo."

I told her we were only playing nice and she said to the lady that she'd be back in a minute and grabbed me by the arm and we dashed into a back room full of shampoo smells. She opened a first-aid kit and put iodine on Pablo's ear, and then a Band-Aid on either side of the hole. He was fixed, but Mom and me were not because she was steaming mad.

"I can't do my work if I have to worry about what trouble you are cookin' up all day long," she said.

"No more trouble," I said. "I'll just sit and play my trumpet. But I've been thinking, can I have one of your hoop earrings for Pablo? You won't let me pierce my ear but since he has a hole . . . "

"I've had it," Mom said. "I've had it up to here." And she held her hand up to her forehead. But there was still an inch to go to the top of her head, so she hadn't *had it* with me completely.

"It's not my fault," I said quietly. "I think my patch wore down."

"The only thing worn down is that excuse," she said right back. "I could plaster you in patches and you would still do the same nutty stuff."

"Don't raise your voice," I said. "You know it upsets Pablo."

I thought she was going to burst into flames she was so mad. "Okay," she said to herself, and shoved her hands into her pockets like she was digging for change. "Take a deep breath. Count to ten. Maybe day care is the answer."

"Maybe I can get a job here with you," I suggested. "I could wash hair."

"You'd put us out of business in a week," she said, starting to come around. "You'd scrub those old-lady heads down to a nub. They'd look like the little bald spot you wore down on your own crown picking and scratching." I touched my head and gave her a hurt face because my bald spot was a sensitive subject.

"I'm sorry," she purred, then grabbed me and gave me a hug and said we'd figure something out.

After she went back to work, Pablo and I marched home. Pablo was fine and as soon as I unlocked the front door we ran to Mom's jewelry box and got a big hoop earring because she hadn't said no, exactly. I put it through Pablo's hole and called him "Pirate Matey Pablo!" Then we turned the couch into a pirate ship. I got a sheet and hoisted it up with the floor lamp and clamped a steak knife between my teeth and we got busy attacking other ships. When Mom came home she caught me sword fighting with my patch over one eye and lipstick blood on my shirt and arms. She sent me to my room to chill out while she mixed a drink.

"Do you feel like your meds are really wearing off?" she asked when she came to check up on me and found me walking on my hands.

"Can I get back to you on that?" I shouted, and fell over.

"Don't play with me that way," she replied, and dropped to her knees and felt under my shirt for the patch, then tickled my belly. "I love you too much to get jerked around by you."

The next day the letter came from Dad's lawyer and that's the last time until the car ride I heard Mom hissing, "Aw, *sugar*, *sugar*, *sugar*!"

I must have fallen asleep in the car because I woke up when it stopped and Mom was tugging on the speaker wire from my tape player like I was a fish she was reeling in.

"Are we there yet?" I asked, and rubbed my ears.

"Almost," she said. "Your dad's place is up the street. I wanted to stop and talk over a few things before we arrive. Most of all I want to say my real goodbye to you now, because when I see your dad and grandma everything is going to be weird and I might be weird too and I don't want you thinking I'm bailing out on you or something." She held me by the cheeks and kissed me like you would a picture in a frame. "Listen to your dad," she said. "He's your dad. But if anything seems out of whack you call me right away and I'll come get you. Okay?" She held my chin in her hands and stared real hard into my eyes before looking toward her purse.

"This is for you," she said, and handed me an envelope folded in half. "There is money in it. Not play money. But emergency money." I opened the envelope. There was a twenty-dollar bill and a page of lined paper with rows of quarters taped to it. She read the puzzled look on my face.

"The quarters are for a pay phone," she explained.

"Can I call you now?" I said. "Because I already think this whole thing is out of whack."

"This is not out of whack," she stressed. "You are starting from scratch with your dad, so everything feels strange." Then she put the car in gear and I knew she was being brave so I didn't say another word. We slowly rolled forward and just up the street Grandma was sitting on a porch smoking, and next to her was a thin man dressed in neatly pressed clothes. He was sweeping the porch but leaned the broom handle against the wall when he saw us.

Mom stopped and waved, then opened her door. I got out as Grandma and Dad scrambled down the steps. Before he said anything to me he tried to kiss Mom but she yanked her head back as if Dad's lips were electrified. Then she gave him a frozen look and said to me, "Joey, go get the luggage out of the trunk."

I got the keys out of the ignition and went around to the back of the car with my head spinning so fast I couldn't pluck one thought out of the blur of them. The two of them being weird together was making me think if I locked myself in the trunk they might forget about being mad at each other and focus on me.

But I canceled that thought. And by the time I came back dragging my army duffel bag no one was talking but they were staring so hard at each other, with their mouths slowly opening and closing like big goldfish, I figured I had gone deaf from bad nerves and started twisting my fingers into my ears like when they needed cleaning.

"Don't worry," Dad finally said. "I'll take good care of him." I heard that loud and clear and by then he was holding the box of patches. "I'll change it every day like I do my nicotine patch, or every other day depending—"

Mom cut him off. "Just follow the prescription," she said sharply. "Joey will tell you."

"Don't worry," he said.

"But I do," Mom replied. "You might mess with *my* head. But if you mess with this kid . . ." She didn't finish her thought out loud because she had finished it in her mind so many times, and it was making her so huffy she was about to lose it. So it was my turn again to help her out.

I reached for her hand and when she glanced over at me I winked our giant eye-squishing secret wink, which was a reminder to chill out. She smiled and instead of going off the deep end, she stooped down by my side, fixed the hair back over my getting-better bald spot, then gave me a hug. "Call me," she whispered in my ear. "Call often so I can say I love you." Then she turned, stiffly marched like a windup toy soldier toward the car, got in, and drove off.

3

STORYBOOK LAND

Mom was disappearing down the road and Dad was shifting around in front of me with his arms and legs crossing back and forth like he was sharpening knives. He was *wired*. No doubt about it. When I looked in a mirror I could see it in my eyes, and now I could see it in his. Even with my medicine working real good, I felt nervous inside he was so hyper. Now I knew what Mom meant when she said he was like me, only *bigger*. He was taller than me too. He had long arms and pointy elbows and a humming sound came out of his body as if he was run by an electric motor. I took a deep breath and even though my insides were churning I was determined to stand there and be as stiff as the rusted-up Tin Man from *The Wizard of Oz*.

"Well, Joey," Dad said with a grin rocking back and

forth on his face like a canoe on high seas, "you can call me Carter." And he stuck out his hand to shake.

I knew I'd never call him that. But before I could call him the one important word I had waited so long to use, Grandma stepped forward.

"Truce," she barked, and stuck out her wrinkled old hand which looked like a dried fish. "Since you're gonna be here for a while we might as well get along."

She had her hair cut short and slicked all the way forward with something so shiny I thought it was covered with Christmas tree tinsel.

"Come on," Grandma persisted, and poked her hand forward again. "Don't make me think you aren't happy to see me."

I squinted back at her because the sun reflected off her hair and directly into my eyes.

"No," I said, and began to say that I was happy to see her, because the last time I saw her she had been walking off down the street and I figured she was washed down the sewer drain where I found her shoe and nothing else, but she jerked her head back before I could say so.

"*No!*" she squawked like a parrot. "Did you say 'no'? Well, I can see already that you have stopped using the good manners *I* taught you when you lived with *me*."

"I have manners," I said, with my voice sounding tight. "Mom makes me use manners. Have I done anything wrong yet? No. Have I said anything mean? No. I'm polite."

I still hadn't moved an inch except for my mouth, which was now all oiled up from defending myself.

Grandma clamped her lips together and turned away to glare over at Carter. "I told you how *that person* lets him run the show," she complained, and gasped for breath. "The cart leadin' the horse!"

Carter kept whipping around and finally an uneven sound came out of his mouth like a car engine that wouldn't start. Then he waved his hand in front of his face as if it were a magic wand and suddenly he went from a stutter to full-speed-ahead talking. "That's all in the past!" he shouted, and pulled Grandma behind him a little too hard. "I've been thinking about what we should do today, and I have the perfect idea." Instantly he was full of energy and happiness, and he smiled real big and announced we were going to Storybook Land Fun Park. "You have to see this place," he said. "It's where my *whole life* turned around."

I wasn't sure what he meant. If his life turned around when he was a kid that would mean it got worse. But if he turned it around as an adult, that would mean he got better.

"Hey, this thing is heavy!" he shouted, lifting my duffel bag. "Whatcha got in here?"

"Clothes, shoes, books, my trumpet," I said, trying

to picture it all like it was on the list Mom made for me.

"Did you bring a baseball glove?" he asked as I followed him up to the porch. " 'Cause I'm coaching a team and I could use a ringer like you."

"No," I replied. "I don't have one."

"Don't sweat it," he said, plopping my duffel bag down inside the front door. "I'll pick one up this week. Now let me see the size of your hand." I held mine up with my fingers spread wide open and he did too. When our hands pressed together I felt a jolt as if he had a joy buzzer in his.

We piled into his big old car and all the way to Storybook Land I imagined playing baseball. I was pretty good at throwing rocks, so I figured I'd be pretty good at pitching. I wanted to tell Dad that I would love to play on his team but I couldn't get a word in.

He just kept talking and talking his nonstop sunny talk about what a great summer we were going to have and that he had tons of plans and that we would get caught up as father and son and soon all our rough past would be behind us and we would have nothing but smooth sailing for our future. And he especially kept talking about Storybook Land. "You gotta, gotta, gotta see this place. Gotta!"

Grandma sat next to him with gray clouds of cigarette smoke over her head as if her grumpy mood had set her hair on fire. Finally, after Dad said "You gotta see it" for the hundredth time, she yelled at him. "Okay, Carter! We're on our way there for god's sake. Give that motormouth of yours a rest!" She was going to say more but she got choked off by a coughing fit.

Dad continued talking his fast talk and when he took a breath I tried to tell him about wanting to play ball on his team, but he cut me off like a clueless driver and kept going so I just listened, which was okay with me because it made him happy. I figured I'd tell him when I had a chance. For now, it was enough that we were together even if he was taking me to a place which was way too young for my age. He was trying to get to know me, so it was fine. We had to start somewhere, and maybe in his mind I was still a baby.

After we got out of the car Grandma announced she would allow Dad and me some time alone to get caught up while she played miniature golf. "Gonna work on my short game," she wheezed, then bent over hacking with her hands on her knees. When she finally pulled herself together and stood up she said, "Should have brought my oxygen tank today. It's smoggy."

"See you later," I said as nicely as I could because she was a handful when she got mad. Dad and I headed down a little stone path lined with flowers and a short white picket fence that wasn't tall enough to keep out the golden squirrels. As we strolled, teenagers passed by dressed up as storybook characters. They waved at us and when they smiled their painted faces wrinkled up into strange masks. We waved back. The wolf from Little Red Riding-Hood howled at some cowering kid who screamed and clutched his mother's pants. Dad nudged me with his elbow and said, "Your granny would eat that old wolf alive!"

"I think so," I said, then added, "but why does she need oxygen?"

"Emphysema," he said. "From smoking. She can't get a whole breath and now needs to carry around one of those little oxygen tanks, but some days she's too embarrassed to do it. I just hope she can get through the golf okay."

"Me too," I said, imagining Granny slumped over the miniature windmill, or halfway down the little wishing well. It wasn't funny.

The first exhibit we came to was the sad-eyed Humpty Dumpty. From Dad's buildup I was expecting something very fancy, but there was only a painted half-cracked concrete egg leaning against a cinder-block wall. All the king's horses and men were made of carved wood and staked into the ground. They were tilted one way or another and splattered with mud.

"This is where it happened," Dad whispered as he squatted down and wiped the figures clean with his handkerchief. "Right at this spot." He drew an X on the ground with his finger. "This is where my *whole life* turned around. I had wandered in here one night after having a few too many drinks, and I passed out and the next thing I knew it was morning and a girl dressed as Little Miss Muffet was waking me up with her shoe and telling me to move on or else she'd call the cops. I stood up and stared over at old Humpty and I thought, I'm as bad as he is. I'm nothing more than a teary-eyed busted-up egg. And as I left the park I thought, Man, I can learn a lesson from that Humpty Dumpty dude. So the next day I came back and just stared at him and the more I stared the less I liked myself. I didn't want to be a pathetic broken egg with everyone trying and failing to put me back together again. I decided on the spot that Humpty was never going to get better. He didn't have the *willpower* to stop whining and get off his can and pull his own self together and move on. Right after that I went to a clinic and dried out, and whenever I get a chance I come to pat and polish old Humpty's head. Believe me, I've been in every clinic in Pittsburgh, but not one of them taught me a lesson more valuable than what I've learned in Storybook Land. You know what I mean?" he said. He turned toward me, and waited for me to say something.

"I think I know what you mean," I said, but I wasn't quite sure if when last year I was sent down to the special-ed school I had become a Humpty Dumpty who had to glue himself back together again. Because I didn't do it myself. I had a lot of good people to help me.

"You know," Dad started up again, flapping his arms around as we strolled along the path past the Three Little Pigs, "this isn't a kiddie park after all. I mean, everything I see here really gets me to *thinking*."

"Dad, can I talk for a while?" I asked.

"Nobody's stopping you," he said. "Two people can talk at once. It's like watching TV and talking. No big deal."

"Yeah, but it's hard for me to do that. I want to listen to you, then I want you to listen to me, and go back and forth like people who want to know about each other."

"Sure, we can do that," he said. "Now, keep talking and we'll go down to Jack and the Beanstalk. Man, that is one place where I really did some *deep* thinking about *you*."

The beanstalk was a telephone pole painted green with wide metal leaves running up both sides. "Check this out," Dad said, and scampered up the pole as if he had done it a hundred times already. At the top was the giant's balcony. Dad stood on it, shaded his eyes with his hands, and shouted, "Fe! Fi! Fo! Fum! I smell the blood of a little one."

I laughed up at him and shaded my eyes too. "Fe! Fi! Fo! Fum!" I boomed. "I smell the blood of a great big bum!"

"Joey," he said, making a sad Humpty face, "there's not a man alive who wouldn't feel some guilt for abandoning his kid. But I'll make it up. I'll think of some way to pay you back for all I've done wrong to you. We were apart for a long time, but from now on, I swear, I'll stick with you. And if you disappear again I'll sniff you out like the giant and track you down."

I stared up at him and he looked huge, as if he could see around the entire world and sniff me out no matter where I was. Half of me loved it because he was saying we would never be lost from each other again. The other half was a little scared because if I wanted to get away from him it meant I couldn't—couldn't run or hide or disappear without him finding me.

"Joey, do you get what I'm saying to you, son? This place made me *think*." He squinted and thumped his forehead with the palm of his hand. "*Think* like never before."

"Dad?" I asked, looking up at him as I stumbled forward. "Can we do something a little more fun now?"

"Yeah, we can take a break from all this thinking," he said. He climbed down the beanstalk and swung me around and nearly snapped my neck. "Sure. Let's go get our pictures taken so we can always remember this day. And then we can go on the bumper cars in the park."

We walked down the path and he continued talking nonstop.

"Now look over there," he said, and pointed at Goldilocks and the Three Bears in their little house. "We can learn so much about each other here. How hot do you like your porridge?"

"What's porridge?" I asked. "I never ate any."

"See!" he declared. "See. Now I know something more about you."

And before I could ask him how he liked his porridge he said, "Okay. Who is smarter? Hansel or Gretel?"

"Hansel," I said. "He tricked the witch with the chicken bone. Who do you—"

"Oh, look," he said. "There's the Old Lady Who Lives in a Shoe. She had so many *accidents* she didn't know what to do. And there goes that kissin' fool, Georgie Porgie. I know how he feels."

I knew how Dad felt about everything. But Dad didn't know how I felt about anything. All the way to the photo booth he kept pointing out storybook characters and he had something important to say about each one, but after a while I stopped listening because he didn't know if I listened or not.

"There it is," I said, and pointed at the picture booth. We went over and I sat on the big Mother

Goose and Dad put his face into the cutout head of the Jack of Hearts. The photographer took two pictures. One for me, and one for him.

"Better get one for your mom too," he reasoned. "So she won't think I got you hanging by your thumbs down in the basement."

I thought that was a good idea, and when the photographer said "Smile" I thought of Mom and got a big lip-curling grin on my face.

"Okay," Dad said, slipping the photos into his top pocket, "let's hurry up 'cause there are a few more important story spots I need you to see."

"What about the bumper cars?" I asked.

"In a minute," he said. "This next thing is important."

We walked down to the Crooked House and right away Dad bent over to one side and began to play as if he was all crooked. "This is me before," he said, with a wavering voice. "All crooked." Then he straightened up like a soldier at attention. "And this is me now. Do you get it? 'There once was a crooked man, who lived in a crooked house. He had a crooked dog—' "

When he said "dog" the breath went out of me like I had drowned on land.

"Oh my god!" I shouted, then sucked in some air. "I left Pablo in the glove box!"

"Who's Pablo?" he asked.

"My Chihuahua," I cried out with my feet hopping

up and down. "I have to call Mom. Where's a phone?" I looked around like there might be a little crooked phone in the crooked man's house.

"Well, why's he in the glove box?"

"Because he got carsick on the radio," I said, and took off running down the path to where I had seen the log-cabin bathrooms and a pay phone.

By the time Dad caught up to me I had the money envelope out of my pocket and was ripping the tape off the quarters and popping them into the phone slot. I didn't know how much money it would take so I figured putting it all in was good.

"She probably hasn't made it back yet," Dad said as he took the phone from my hand and hung up. All the money came shooting out of the change return and went rolling across the floor.

"I have to go home!" I said as I scrambled for the coins. "What if Pablo is stuck in the glove box when Mom returns the car and Pablo is trapped in there and dies like those kids trapped in car trunks?"

"Joey," Dad said. "Don't turn into a Humpty Dumpty on me. You have to tough it out, buddy. Everything is going to be all right. Why, I bet your mom found Pablo after a while and turned around and brought him back. I bet he's on the front porch right now waiting for you."

"Let's go see," I said nervously. "Let's go now."

Dad took my hand and we went running toward

the miniature golf course. Grandma was sitting on a small brown-and-white polka-dotted mushroom seat with her golf club across her knees. "I'm just takin' a breather," she whispered harshly.

"We have to go home," Dad said, and reached for her elbow to get her on her feet and going. "Joey lost his Chihuahua."

"What Chihuahua?" she asked. "Nobody told me a fancy rat dog was part of this deal."

Dad didn't say anything. Instead he scooped her up into his arms. I was already heading for the car and I wished I had the keys because I'd start it up and take off looking for Mom and Pablo.

All the way back to the house Granny said mean things about my "fancy Mexican rat dog."

"He's half-Chihuahua and half-dachshund," I said.

"Half-rat, half-wiener, you mean," she snorted back.

Finally, I couldn't take it anymore and said, "You be quiet."

"No. You be quiet," she shot back.

"No! You be quiet," I said again.

"No. You be quiet," she wheezed.

We kept this up until we pulled into the driveway and I jumped out and there was Pablo on the porch shivering with the handle of his leash fastened around the front-door knob. Mom had written "Miss you already!" in lipstick on the little diamond-shaped window. I grabbed Pablo and kissed him all over his pointy face and he kissed me back with his awful dog-puke breath, but I didn't care. I loved him and he loved me, and that's all that mattered.

"See," Dad said, coming up from behind me, "I was right, wasn't I?"

He was. I set Pablo down and threw my arms around Dad's neck and just hugged him as tightly as I could because he was totally right and didn't turn into a busted-up Humpty Dumpty when I had.

"How did you know he'd be here?" I said.

"Hey, what are dads for?" he replied all jolly, and hoisted me up over his shoulder like a sack of flour, and we entered the house while Grandma and Pablo growled at each other. I figured they were going to have a heck of a time because neither of them ever backed down from anyone or anything.

"Hey, Dad," I said while I had the chance. "I want to play baseball."

"That's my boy," he said. "A chip off the old block." Then he kept talking and I stopped listening.

4

BAD GOLF

In the morning Dad came in my room. I was happy to see him because I had been awake most of the night from Grandma's coughing attacks. She would sputter and spit for a while until it sounded like she had dredged up a hair ball from deep inside. Afterward she'd clear her throat and finally settle down. Then, just as I was drifting back to sleep, she'd start up all over again. Finally I got up and turned on my tape player, but the batteries had worn out so I couldn't escape her awful sounds and spent hours chewing my fingernails down to the part of the skin that tasted like baby carrots.

"How's your patch?" Dad asked, and sat on the edge of my bed with my box of patches. "You need a change before I head out to work?"

"Yup," I replied, and turned my book facedown on

the bedside table. "And you better leave another one with me just in case." I was thinking that I would be alone with Grandma all day and might need some extra meds to help.

"The box says one at a time," he said. He pulled a patch out of his shirt pocket and gave it to me. "One more thing," he added. "I need to draw your foot so I can get you the right size baseball cleats."

He put a piece of paper on the floor and I stepped on it. "By the way," he asked, looking up at me as he drew the outline with a pencil, "you throw left or right?"

"Left," I replied. "Catch right."

He smiled. "Excellent. We could use a lefty pitcher."

He stood up and folded the paper. "Hey," he said before slipping out the door. "I told Grandma to make you some porridge, not too hot." He grinned. I grinned too, and then he was gone, but I still had my grin.

As soon as he left I peeled the covers all the way down and searched for Pablo. He had a bad habit of chewing a hole in the sheet and digging a burrow in the mattress. I think he was part prairie dog too. When I found him I lifted him up and we danced around. "I'm bad! I'm mad! I'm a hundred percent of Mom and Dad," I sang. It was my favorite song and Pablo liked it too. But I couldn't swing him around too much or he'd throw up.

I got dressed and when I looked into the mirror on the back of the door to fix my hair, I saw that I was still grinning. So far, so good, I thought. He's happy, and I'm happy. Then I remembered I had to spend the whole day with Grandma.

I decided, on the spot, that I was going to be nice to her. I figured it was my choice to set the mood. She was always going to be her two selves—one nice and funny, and the other mean and scary. She wouldn't change, because she never felt that anything she did was wrong. So all the changing was up to me, and that was okay because I knew I could be wrong most of the time. So, I'd start off with my best foot forward. And if she was mean, then I'd stay nice for as long as I could until she wore me out and I'd go hide.

I put my hand on the doorknob, took a deep breath, and opened the door. When Pablo and I entered the kitchen Grandma was prying a stuck Pop-Tart out of the toaster with a butter knife.

"How'd you sleep?" she asked. Her voice was hoarse.

"You should unplug the toaster before you stick a knife in," I said, trying to be helpful. "Once I did what you are doing and got a shock that knocked me off the counter."

"Well, I'm already half dead," she replied, "so a little shock will only pep me up."

"That's why I eat vitamins," I said.

She frowned. "Now, how many Pop-Tarts do you want? And how many does that dog eat?"

"We need to buy some dog food," I replied. "And Dad said you were making me porridge. Like the Three Bears."

"He's just a big talker," she said. "Better get used to his gibber-jabber or he'll drive you nuts."

"Can I call my mom?" I asked.

"Why don't you write her a letter?" Grandma said. "A stamp is a lot cheaper than a call."

"Mom gave me money for the phone," I said.

"What do you want to tell her?" Grandma asked.

"That Pablo is okay and that I found him on the porch." I gave him a little squeeze and he made a sound like bagpipes warming up.

"You don't think someone would steal that mongrel?" she said, pointing the knife at Pablo.

"Stop calling him names," I said. "He's a Chihuahua mix. Besides, Mom said—"

"I don't want to hear what your mom has to say on the subject. Just call her and get it over with," she said, then bit down on a piece of burnt Pop-Tart. But she was panting so hard from talking too mean and fast that she had to turn and spit it into the sink so she could take a deep breath off her oxygen hose, which she had hooked to the top of a skinny green tank that was on the counter.

The phone was screwed to the kitchen wall and when I picked it up Grandma began to whistle to herself like she didn't want to hear what I had to say, but I knew she would be listening to every word.

Mom was already at work so I called her there.

"Beauty and the Beast Hair Salon," Tiffany, the receptionist, said.

"This is Joey," I whispered with my hand wrapped around the voice piece. "Is my mom there?"

"One sec', hon," she said, then I heard her yell, "Fran, it's your kid. Sounds like he's been kidnapped."

I heard quick steps. "Hey," Mom said. "Are you all right?"

"I'm fine," I said. "And Pablo is too. I couldn't believe I forgot him."

"Well, I wasn't a mile down the road before he began pitching a fit in the glove box, so it was no big deal to turn around."

"We were at Storybook Land," I said. And then she started asking so many questions about Dad and Grandma and me that I was saying "yes" and "no" and "no" and "yes" like I was playing Ping-Pong with my words.

"Well, have a good day," she said. "It's slow here so I'm dyeing my hair red and getting a pedicure. I'm going to paint my toenails to match my hair and buy a nice pair of summer sandals. You'll hardly know me when you return."

"Pablo will sniff you out," I said.

"Gotta run," she cut in. "The dye is leaking down into my eyes and it stings like the blazes."

"One more thing," I said, raising my voice so that Grandma could hear even if she was deaf, "Dad is real nice. We had fun and he's putting me on his baseball team. He's buying me a glove and cleats."

"Great," she said. "I'm happy to hear that. Now, call me later. Love you." And she hung up.

When I turned around Grandma was leaning back against the kitchen counter with her arms folded across her front. She was eyeing me up and down while taking deep breaths off her oxygen hose.

"I'm glad to have a few hours alone with you," she said in a voice that was like being sent to the principal. "I'd like to set you straight on some things around here before you get any big ideas. Things in this house aren't exactly the same as Carter said they are."

"What do you mean?" I asked, and leaned over to give Pablo a piece of Pop-Tart.

"Oh, he's got a steady job but he still sneak-drinks now and again and he's got himself a girlfriend that hasn't figured out what a loose screw he is. Just know that he hasn't turned into the squeaky-clean Boy Scout he says he is, even though he's a neat-freak." She pointed to the Pop-Tart crumbs. "He'll blow his top if he finds crumbs on the floor," she warned.

"Are you trying to scare me?" I asked as I stooped down and picked them up.

"No, I just want you to know what you're stepping into here. It's been no picnic livin' with him and every day I think I should've stuck it out with you and your mom."

"I thought you slipped down the sewer," I said. "I found your shoe by the grate."

"I hopped a bus," she said. "But I was lookin' for that shoe." She laughed, then her laughter turned into a fit of coughing and she bent over. When she straightened up she raised one finger and held it in front of my face. "A word to the wise," she said. "Don't blab to your mom everything that goes on around here if you want some time with your dad. 'Cause if she knew what all takes place in that man's head, she'd pick you up in the bat of an eye and you'd never see him again."

"I think I need to change my patch," I said. I grabbed Pablo off the floor and speed-walked back to my room. Maybe Dad had done some bad things in the past, I thought as I opened my shirt and reached around to the back of my shoulder and ripped off the patch. But just like me, he deserved a second chance, and I wanted to make up my own mind about him. Then I put the new patch on in a slightly different spot and rubbed it for a minute to heat it up and get it going.

"You can't hide from me all day," Grandma called out, and rapped on the door. "I got big plans for us."

"What?" I yelled. I didn't know where to put my old patch so I stuck it inside the book I was reading.

"Golf," she yelled back. "Now let's get a move on."

I opened the door and stared at her. She had rigged herself up to her oxygen tank, which was stuffed into a blue shoulder bag. The yards of clear plastic hose from the top of the tank ran underneath her shirt and out the back of her collar. It split into two separate lines that curled over her ears and joined at a nose piece that clipped onto the thin wall of flesh between the nostrils. Little jets of air whistled up her nose. The whole thing sort of looked like a costume from a science-fiction movie.

"Don't laugh," she warned me. "Or I'll swat you with this 2-iron."

There was nothing to laugh at. It seemed pretty awful to me because if someone turned the oxygen up she'd swell out and pop like a balloon.

"Believe it or not," she said, "I've been looking forward to your coming. Your dad makes fun of me when I hook this thing up. He said I look like one of those life-support patients. So I don't use it and half the time when I go to do anything I'm just panting like an old hound dog."

"What do you want to do?" I asked.

"If you are anything like your old self you need to run around for a while, so I got a plan that will suit both of us. Now grab my tank. We'll go over to the park and I'll hit a few balls to you."

"Okay," I said. I wasn't sure I could say no.

I followed her out to the front porch. "Help me get into my buggy," she said, pointing to a grocery cart on the sidewalk with an old couch cushion on the bottom. I must have looked confused because she kicked a small stepladder on the porch and said, "Use this. I did have a little handcart for the oxygen but Carter said it cost too much to rent so now he just gets me the tank with the shoulder case and because it's so heavy I can't get very far."

I put the stepladder next to the cart and steadied it with one hand and her with the other as she climbed in. I lifted her oxygen tank up over the edge and set it in her lap. I put the tin bucket of old golf balls between her feet and slid the 2-iron in by her side.

"Don't forget to fold the stepladder up and slide it underneath," she instructed, "or I'll never get out."

After I did that I grabbed Pablo and strapped him into the baby seat, then pushed them down the sidewalk and turned onto the road as Grandma adjusted her little sun umbrella.

"You know, I could always read your mind, Joey," she started up. Her voice was sharp enough to cut through the rattle of the cart on the asphalt. "I could always look into those spinnin' eyes of yours and know what you had cookin' up behind them."

"I don't know what you mean," I said, but right away I noticed my hands were shaking and I felt a little antsy.

"I know you think you can get your mom and dad back together again. Don't tell me I'm wrong, because there's not a kid alive who doesn't think they can get their parents back together once they split up. But do yourself a favor and forget about it. Those two should be apart."

"I only came to visit Dad," I said.

"I hope that's true. But just the other day he said it's his dream to get a whole family together."

My heart started pounding because Grandma said something that I had joked about with Mom. In the car Mom told me to forget about her ever liking Dad again. Ever. But now the idea that Dad secretly wanted the family together only confused me. I didn't know what to say so I changed the subject back to golf.

"How's your game?" I asked.

"Pretty good since I've been working regular on it. Your dad went and got me a starter set of clubs with all the cigarette coupons I saved up. I can't tell if he's being nice to me or if he wants me to exercise myself to the grave."

I didn't know what to say to that either so I kept quiet.

When we reached the park I could only push the cart a few feet into the grass before the wheels stuck. I got the stepladder and helped her out over the side. Then I set the oxygen tank in the front corner of the cart so she could have a few feet of tubing to move around like an astronaut walking in space.

"Run out there for about fifty yards," she said, pointing, "and I'll hit some to you."

"Do I get a helmet?" I asked, as I unstrapped Pablo and set him down.

"No," she said. "Just don't let them hit your noggin. If you go home with a dent in your precious head your mother will have a cow."

"What about my eyes?"

"Put these on," she said, and tossed her pink old-lady sunglasses at me. "Now, no more questions. Just get going."

"Come on, Pablo," I shouted, and we took off across the grass. I had to run with one hand holding the glasses against my face because they were so big they fit like circus clown glasses. When I looked over my shoulder, Grandma was turning off her oxygen tank with one hand and holding a cigarette in the other. I figured in about thirty seconds she'd be ready to ricochet a ball off my head.

The moment we got about fifty yards out Pablo had to go. He tramped around in a little circle, then squatted down. His whole body began to vibrate like he was pooping on the North Pole. I looked up at Grandma. She was smiling, then she aimed the head of her club at us, reared back, and teed off.

"Hurry up, Pablo," I advised as the ball landed about ten yards away. "She's a pretty good shot."

I heard her hit another one. I looked up into the air but the ball was lost in the whiteness of a cloud. Then, *thunk!* It hit a little closer. Pablo stuck his butt up into the air as he finished his business.

"Hurry, you don't want her to hit a hole in one," I said. "Now get a move on." He did, then ran around in figure eights.

Once I got used to spotting the balls in the sky it was easy to catch up to them. I let them hit the ground, then I'd throw them back to where she could reach them with her club and tee up again.

Every time Grandma had a cigarette she turned her oxygen off, and every time she finished one she turned it back on. We kept this up for almost an hour. I liked being outside, running around in the grass with Pablo. It was just the kind of activity Mom was hoping to provide for me. And I wished she was here to see that not everything with Grandma was awful.

I had just picked up a ball when I looked toward Grandma to get ready for her next shot. She raised the golf club back up over her head and in an instant I saw that her oxygen tube had looped around the head of the club.

"Don't swing!" I shouted.

She went into her swing with a smile on her face, maybe because Pablo had stopped to rest and she had him lined up in her sights, when suddenly the club hit the ball and at the same time ripped the oxygen clip clean out of her nose. Her head jerked forward, and she stumbled and fell to her knees.

The ball whistled over my head as I ran toward her. By the time I got there she had hoisted herself up with the club and was standing with her hands on her hips. A little stream of blood was slithering down her upper lip and around the corner of her mouth. The sun made the blood very shiny.

"Of all the brainless, cockeyed things I've ever done this beats the pants off 'em all!" she snapped.

"Are you okay?" I asked. "You're bleeding."

She ran her hand over her mouth. "Don't ever live to be old," she said to me, "or you'll have lived to regret it. I promise you." Then she bent over and began to cough like she would never stop and the nosebleed spattered all over her face and it looked like she had been in a fight. Pablo saw the blood and was going nuts.

"Sit down," I said to her.

"No, or I'll never get up again," she replied between huge gasps for breath. "Just get me home." And then with what sounded like her last breath ever she said, "Shut that yapping rat up."

"Hush," I said to Pablo. "It's not good manners to laugh at other people's mistakes."

"How do you know he's laughing?" she wheezed.

He wasn't laughing. But I didn't want to tell her that the sight of blood made him hysterical.

I picked up the oxygen clip and gave it to her. She gripped it between her teeth and breathed until she began to settle down. I gathered the rest of the balls and put them and the club back into the cart, then I got her up the stepladder and comfy on her little cushion. I grunted and groaned and pushed and pulled the cart out of the grass and back onto the asphalt and we headed for home.

When we got there I led Grandma into the bathroom. "Sit on the toilet seat," I said. "I'll clean you up." I opened the medicine chest and found a plastic bottle of peroxide. I poured it on some tissue and wiped it around her nose and upper lip as she flinched left and right. It was just a little cut. But she said it hurt a lot.

"I need a rest," she said, sounding tired. "I can't do as much as I used to. It's a good thing I don't have you to chase around all day anymore." Then she stood and shuffled over to the couch to take a nap.

I know that when I'm around crazy people it can bring out the craziness in me. But I was telling myself that my medication helps keep me calm, and that no matter who I was around, it was up to me to take a deep breath and still make good decisions for myself. That's what I was thinking as I sneaked into Dad's room. I wanted to see what it looked like and if he had put the Storybook photo of me on his dresser. As I looked around I noticed everything was in its perfect place. The pennies, nickels, and dimes were neatly stacked in columns. Little boxes of matches were lined up in a row like dominoes. There was a small jar of toothpicks and a matching one for Q-Tips. But there was no picture of me, just one of a tall red-haired woman in a baseball uniform. She was waving a bat over her head as if she was going to swat the photographer. Next to that was a baseball sitting on something like a golf tee, so I picked it up. I didn't think Dad would mind if I practiced my throwing.

I walked out back and threw it from one side of the yard to the other. I picked targets to hit like old cans, broken flowerpots, an empty bird house, and sprinklers. I liked doing it because I was good at it, and hitting something over and over again kept me from thinking about what Grandma had said about Dad trying to get the family together.

When Dad came home he found me in the yard. He was holding two baseball gloves and tossed one to me. "Try it on," he said, smiling and rocking his head back and forth. I worked my fingers up into the holes and it felt like a good fit.

"Now hold it over your face and smell it," he said.

I did.

"Have you ever smelled anything better?"

"Nothing," I said, and smelled it again.

"Now go over to the other side of the yard and throw me one as hard as you can."

I did. I reared back and let it fly and it smacked when it hit his glove. "Wow," he said, "that was some heat." But when he pulled the ball out of his glove his eyes got big. "Where'd you get this ball?" he asked.

"Your room," I said quietly because I didn't know if I was allowed in his room.

"Well, this is my signed Roberto Clemente ball."

"So?" I said.

"Does your mother keep you hidden under a rock?" he asked. "You don't know who Clemente is?"

"I just don't play much with other kids," I said. "They tease me."

He stared intensely at me for a moment, like he was trying to make up his mind to be mad or not. Then that big canoe smile floated out over his mouth.

"Well, I'm sure Roberto won't mind training the next Cy Young winner," he said, tossing the ball at me and punching his fist into his glove. "Right in the pocket," he said. "Bring Roberto home to Papa."

I leaned way back then fired another one across the yard, right at the spot he punched. *Smack!*

"Wow," he said again. "Don't you worry about kids teasing you. From now on they're gonna be hounding you for an autograph. You have an arm like a cannon, dude."

"Told you I was good at throwing stuff," I said.

"Can you hit?" he asked.

"Don't know," I said. "I never tried that part of it."

"Well, we'll find out tomorrow," he said. "I'll take you to a game."

"I called Mom today and told her I was on your team."

"How is she?" he asked, tossing me the ball.

"Great," I said as it slapped into my glove. "She's dyeing her hair red."

Dad arched his eyebrows and his canoe smile rocked back and forth across his face. "She was always a sharp-looking redhead," he said, "and I sure do have a thing for redheads." Then he sort of looked a little lost like he was missing her. I was going to throw the ball again, but I was afraid it would bounce off his head, so I let him think for a while.

5

CAVEMAN

"I want a cigarette so bad," Dad said, "I can taste it." He pulled up his T-shirt sleeve, ripped the nicotine patch off his shoulder, and stuck it on the dashboard. "I don't know why we wear these darn patches," he said. "They don't do a thing for me."

As he reached above his sun visor and pulled out a pack of cigarettes, I spotted the death-skull tattoo on his arm where the patch had been.

"I want one of those," I said, and pointed at it.

He glanced at his shoulder and frowned. "That's one patch that's *never* coming off," he said, and shook a cigarette toward his lips.

"Maybe I can get a tattoo of a patch and then I'll never have to change my meds again," I said, joking around.

"Well, I've about had it with this patch business," he

said. "This is what works for me." He lit the cigarette and inhaled. "Sometimes the disease is better than the medicine. You know what I mean? When I was working down in Panama, a doctor gave me some kind of anti-malaria pills and said, 'Now don't use them unless you have to, 'cause they'll probably kill you before they cure you.' "

I wanted to talk about tattoos but he was already talking his talk. I knew I should listen because that's how you get to know someone when you haven't spent a lot of time together, but other things were on my mind. I was thinking that being away from Mom made me feel different. Like there was one Joey for Mom and a different Joey for Dad and that I was becoming two Joeys. Mom's Joey didn't want a tattoo but Dad's Joey did.

"Dad, have you ever felt like two people at once?" I asked.

He didn't answer. Instead he exhaled and said, "You know, I never had much interest in kids. But after my last arrest I had to do community service, and the coaching opportunity was way better than picking trash on the side of the road with a bunch of jittery winos, so now I'm the coach of a team of Police Athletic League kids. You know, local kids who if they didn't play ball might get into a little summer trouble. So you shouldn't be afraid of them."

I wasn't afraid of them. I was sort of afraid of him.

He was already a criminal. "Why were you arrested?" I asked.

He turned and smiled at me, then turned away and flicked his cigarette butt out the window. "The usual charge," he said. "Stupidness. Just plain old stupidness."

"Really?" I said, unsure. "I thought you had to *do* something stupid to be arrested. Not just *be* stupid."

"Well, that's true," he said. "I did something stupid."

"What?"

"I bit a man."

"You mean like a dog?"

"Yeah, pretty much just like a dog."

"Where'd you bite him?"

"The nose," he said, and held the tip of his reddish nose, then rubbed it between his thumb and finger like he was polishing it.

"Wow!" I said, squirming in my seat. "Wow! Do you know why I was kicked out of school and sent to special-ed school?"

"No," he said. "What Pigza stupidness did you do?"

"I accidentally cut off a girl's nose tip with a pair of scissors. I was running with them and tripped over her and just snipped a tiny bit of her nose off. Can you believe that? Did you trip too?"

"Nope," he said, and lit another cigarette. "I didn't trip. I flipped. I was in a bar and a guy snatched my beer and drank it all down and I got so mad I just grabbed him by the ears and bit his nose before he could pull away."

"You mean yours wasn't an accident?" I said, and I kept looking at his sharp yellow teeth as if he were the Big Bad Wolf.

"No," he replied. "Nope. You know, Joey, I know you want to have long father-to-son talks with me, and it's not that I don't want to have long talks with you but you have to realize I really only want to talk about the future with you. Not the past. My past is not good, Joey, so I don't have the good ol' days to feel all warm and fuzzy about. My past, like the nose thing, gets sort of scary and ugly, and to tell you the truth I'd just rather have, you know, the new times to talk about. The *now* times. I'd rather just show you Storybook Land and play baseball and work on making new memories."

"Don't you even want to talk about what happened with Mom?" I asked.

"No," he replied. "Definitely not. Because the worst thing I ever did was mess your mom up and it just makes me feel sick to think about it."

"But I was awful to her too," I said. "Like, a million times. And she forgave me each and every time."

"Well, we may have that nose problem in common, but not the Mom forgiveness deal. She won't have a thing to do with me," he said.

"Grandma told me it was your secret dream to have a family again," I ventured.

"Grandma can't keep a secret," he said. "She's yappier than Pablo. Sure, I might have said that. But then after I have a few beers I'm liable to say anything—I'm one of those drinkers that for every bottle of beer I empty, I fill it back up with tears."

We pulled into the Police Athletic League ball-field parking lot, which was right behind the backstop.

"Dad," I said, smiling. "I think we just had our first back-and-forth conversation."

"I'm sure we'll have more," he said, looking out onto the field, and I could tell he was already distracted. He pulled his patch off the dashboard and slapped it back onto his shoulder, then swung his door open. "But for now, we have a game to play, and I have to knock these kids into shape. Why don't you take a seat in the dugout and just watch while I get some drills going." He went around to the trunk, opened it, and pulled out a big bag of bats and balls.

"About tonight," he said. "I don't think you'll be playing, but don't feel bad. You'll be the new kid on the team and I have to use the regulars, but if I get a chance I'll put you in so keep an eye on the game." Then he reached out and tousled my hair with his hand and I loved it. Loved it more than anything he had said.

Suddenly he yelled out over his shoulder at the team. "Okay, you slackers, pick up the pace! You don't want to be losers for your entire lives, do you?" Then he began hitting sharp ground balls in their direction which scattered them like pigeons.

After a few minutes of feeling out of place over nothing in particular I began to entertain myself as best I could. I got a pen out of the car and drew a skull tattoo on my shoulder. I took out my shoelaces and relaced them in the fancy way Dad had his laced. Some kid had left behind a bag of peanuts and I took a few and opened them up while I whistled "Peanuts" from the Tijuana Brass tape. I shoved a peanut up one nostril and covered the other with a finger. I snorted as hard as I could and the peanut blasted from its hole like a rocket from a bazooka. I fired a few at Dad as he trotted by and one of them hit him in the back of the neck and he slapped at it like it was a bug.

I had just shoved a peanut up my nose when a tall red-haired woman in a baseball uniform walked into the dugout with a big equipment bag slung over her shoulder. For a moment I thought Mom had snuck up on me. "So," she said, and dropped the bag on the bench which kicked up a cloud of dust, "are you the new ringer Carter told me about?"

"I'm not sure," I said with my voice buzzing like a kazoo because of the peanut vibrating in my nose. "I haven't played yet, so I don't know."

"Well, you can't take the field until you have the right equipment," she said. She unzipped the bag and reached into it, and while she did that I fake-sneezed the peanut into my hand.

"Bless you," she said.

"Thanks," I replied. "Want a peanut?" I held it out toward her on my palm. It looked a little slimy.

"Did that come out of your nose?" she asked, and squinted at me with her hands on her hips. "Your dad does the same thing. He puts them up his nose and shoots them out at people. But usually he has a few drinks first. Have you been drinking?"

"No," I said. "Never. But Dad and I do have a lot in common." I tossed the peanut over the fence. "Never mind about the snack," I said, and rubbed my hands together. "I was just trying to be polite."

She shrugged, then pulled a jersey out of her bag. "I believe this is for some kid named Pigza." She handed it to me.

I unfolded it. On the tar-black front was printed STEEL CITY SPORTS in thick yellow ink, like what they use on highway lines. I turned it over. J. PIGZA was printed across the back above a big number 17. "How did you know this was my lucky number?" I asked.

"I have some inside information," she said, and nodded toward Dad, who was scolding some kid for loving his mother too much.

"And you'll need a cap too," the lady said. She reached into the bag and handed one to me. S.C.S. was sewn onto the front in shiny gold thread. "And cleats. Are these the right size?"

They were. "Yes," I said.

Then she pulled out the best thing I had ever seen. It was a black sweatband with a yellow number 17 on it. "That's not for your wrist," she said to me. "I understand you have a little buddy—you can slide this around his belly."

"This is so cool," I said, and just stared at it. "Pablo will love it."

"Now put your jersey on," she said. "You can't get into the game without an official PAL jersey."

I yanked my shirt up over my head like it was covered with red ants. I put on my jersey and smoothed it against my flat belly and breathed in the rubbery smell of the lettering.

"You need baseball pants," she said. "Carter forgot to tell me."

I looked down at my jeans.

"You can wear what you have on, but to look really sharp you have to get the matching pants. What waist do you wear?"

"I don't know," I said.

She leaned forward and put her thumb on my belly button, then kept reaching around me until she got some measurement. "Skinny," she said. "You need to fatten up a bit."

"Like Hansel?"

"In a way," she said. "It's just if you play the game you need a couple extra pounds. I think your Dad is going to have to put you on a large-pizza-a-day diet."

I grinned. I loved pizza. "Extra cheese and extra vegetables!" I sang like I was ordering one over the phone.

"Your wish is my command," she sang back, and pulled a phone out of her pocket and dialed. "Hello. I'd like to order a pizza for delivery. Yeah. Extra cheese and extra vegetables. Yeah. What?"

Dad was yelling at some kid to pay attention or else he'd bury him up to his neck and use his head for second base. She held her hand over the phone and hollered, "Hey, Carter. Shut your trap! I'm ordering a pizza."

Dad turned around with his mouth open.

"That's right," she said. "Put a sock in it." Then she returned to the phone. "The PAL field over by Clemente Memorial. Yeah. Steel City Sports. Cash. Okay." Then she hung up.

"By the way," she said, and stuck out her hand, "I'm Leezy Fiddle, the sports store sponsor for your team and the gal that keeps your dad from going around the bend every game day."

"Nice to meet you," I said.

"I'll be seeing more of you," she replied. "Right now, I better go chill down the coach before his head pops."

Dad was threatening to wrap masking tape around some kid's eyes and make him "play by instinct! Like a freakin' Luke Skywalker!"

Leezy walked over and stood behind him. She was taller than he was and slapped the brim of his cap down over his eyes. He whipped around like he was going to fight, but by then she was trotting into the outfield to catch fly balls.

When the game began Dad started out all calm and helpful, but I knew it wouldn't last because watching him was like watching a big version of my old wired self. He gathered all the players around him. "Okay," he said, "we can whip these guys. We can show 'em who the losers are. We can win this easy and get back into second place. Now, let's play *ball*!"

Then he twisted the game ball into the pitcher's glove. "Virgilio, just throw heat. That's all it takes. High, hard heat. The last time they slaughtered your change-up. This time only heat. Got that? Nothing fancy. Remember, a cannon doesn't need a curve or a slider or a fork ball—it just does one thing well—it fires heat. Now go out there and show them you got a cannon for an arm."

Virgilio silently nodded along until Dad slapped him

on the back, and then he ran toward the mound as if he had been shot out of a cannon.

"Batter up," the umpire shouted the moment he finished sweeping off home plate.

Immediately Dad started pacing back and forth and shouting at the other team's players. "No batter!" he yelled. "Batter's got a limp stick!"

Virgilio leaned forward and sort of threw an overhand lob.

"Ballll," mooed the ump.

"Ball on what planet?" Dad hollered.

The catcher threw the ball back to Virgilio harder than Virgilio had thrown it at the plate. I hadn't played before but I knew the pitcher should be throwing harder than the catcher.

"Now show him the *cannon*!" Dad roared at Virgilio. "Put some smoke on it!"

Virgilio threw the same slow pitch.

"Ballll two," the umpire called.

Dad jumped into the air. "Ball?" he shouted. "A Seeing Eye dog knows that's a strike."

On Virgilio's next pitch the batter slammed the ball into the outfield for a double.

"I said throw heat, Son. *Heat!*" Dad screamed. "This isn't T-ball."

The next batter hit a double and drove in the first batter. The following batter cracked one up the middle and Virgilio skipped out of the way and fell onto his side.

"Come on," Dad groaned. "Show some bad intentions out there on the mound. Imagine you are throwing a brick through your teacher's window."

It must have been a heavy brick in Virgilio's mind. He lobbed it in there and the kid hammered it over the fence.

"Ouch," Leezy said, and winced. She got up off the bench to try and calm Dad down because he was hopping from foot to foot while calling Virgilio and the umpire a bunch of names and the coach on the other team was yelling back that this was a family activity and for Dad to "watch his language" or he'd report him to the front office. By then Leezy had her arm around Dad and I was glad she was bigger than him and she began to steer him around by his head like he was a calf she was going to wrestle to the ground and tie up with a rope.

By the time Virgilio got out of the inning we were down seven runs. He took a seat at the end of the bench and pulled his jersey up over his head and didn't move a muscle until he had to pitch again. At the end of the fourth inning we were down fifteen to zip.

"Okay, Pigza," Dad said, and tossed me the ball. "Show them what *heat* means."

"Me?" I said.

"Yeah, you," Dad replied, and he pulled me to one

side. "One thing before you take the mound," he said. "I have to give you my special 'pitchers only' pep talk." He put his arm around me and walked me away from the other players. "Okay," he continued, "this is all you ever need to know about baseball. It is a game as old as the moment men went from animal to human and started hating each other. It comes down to this—a caveman with a stick versus a caveman with a rock. And you are the caveman with the rock. Remember, the rock rules. The rock is always in control of the situation. The caveman with the stick can't do a thing as long as you control the rock. Now, get out there and show him who the superior caveman is." Then he slapped me across the butt and before I knew it I was trotting out to the mound and I had no idea what I was going to do.

As I cut across the grass infield a kid in the other dugout yelled, "Mystery pitcher!"

I was a mystery, and I liked it. I stood on the mound and looked out at both dugouts and all the people sitting in the stands. Half of them wanted me to mess up, and half of them wanted me to succeed. It was about the same as being back in school, where some of the kids were hoping I'd get better and the others just wanted me to do something screwy to drive the teacher nuts and stop the lesson.

I always had people rooting for me both ways. I didn't realize it was preparing me for baseball.

"Okay," the catcher yelled. "Put 'er in here," and he punched his glove with his fist to give me a target. The batter was ready so I just reared back and threw one as hard as I could, and you could hear the clang of the ball as it hit the umpire right in his wire mask.

"Ball one," the ump croaked as he staggered back and adjusted his mask.

"That's my kid who threw that heater!" Dad hollered as he swung his arms over his head. Then he cupped his hands around his big mouth and yelled at the other coach. "Watch out for my kid! He's a caveman." Then he turned to me. "Show 'em what you got, Pigza!"

My next pitch kicked up the dirt around the batter's feet and he danced all the way to the backstop. From that moment on I knew he was afraid of me. I was the caveman with the rock and all he could do was stand there and wait while I squinted in at the catcher as if I couldn't see far enough to tie my shoe. My third pitch hit the catcher in the knee and he toppled over in agony. I was getting closer. Then I reared so far back that my hand nearly touched the ground and I sprang forward and threw a smoker right down the middle.

"Strike!" the ump called out.

Once I got the target lined up the batter didn't have a chance. I struck him out on two more pitches. Then I threw six more pitches and we were out of the inning. It was pretty easy for me, and when I trotted off the field Dad was beaming and his canoe smile was sailing the seven seas.

"Awesome heat," he said. "You blew them away, caveman. You crushed them. Wow! Now give me five," and he held his hand palm out.

I wound up like I was pitching and slapped his hand as hard as I could, which must have stung him a lot harder than it did me because I knew it was coming.

"Now you give me five," I said, and held out my hand. By the steamed look on his face I knew he wanted to really get me back, and when he swung his hand down full-force I pulled mine away at the last second. He lunged forward and lost his balance and stumbled for a few steps before he grabbed the chain-link fence and held himself up.

By then I was doubled up and howling with laughter like a spotted hyena, and Leezy and a bunch of the guys who saw what I had done were laughing too and Dad just had to bite his lip and settle down. I could tell he didn't think it was funny at all, but I thought it was one of the funniest things I had ever done. I looked over at the team and I could tell they liked me after they saw their crazy coach get tricked by his own kid. I always had a way of getting people on my side.

"I'll get you back," Dad said, trying not to sound too mean, but his face was red. "You watch yourself."

"Sorry," I said in a small voice.

"Enough fun and games," Dad said, once he had

pulled himself together. "We're down fifteen runs. If we don't score some runs this inning the ump will call the game short because we're getting blown out. So let's show some backbone. Get out there and hit some balls hard."

The first batter was a tall kid with a small face named Defoe who stood like a praying mantis at the plate. He struck out. But the second guy got a base hit. The next guy walked. The next guy walked. The bases were loaded and the next guy struck out without ever taking a swing.

"Oh, for the love of Pete!" Dad yelled at the kid when he scuffed back to the dugout. "What were you doing up there? Meditating?"

Suddenly everyone was looking around. "Next batter," the ump yelled over at Dad.

"Joey," Dad said, and smiled at me because he was still waiting to get me back. "You're next. Now show 'em you're double trouble. A pitcher and a hitter. Come on. Score some runs and save us from feeling like a bunch of losers."

"I've never hit before," I said.

Virgilio held out his bat. "Use this," he suggested, "before your dad uses it on me."

"Don't listen to him," I whispered to Virgilio. "His own mother even says he's all mouth."

I went out to the plate and stood with my toes touching the edge of it.

"You better stand back a foot or so," the ump said, "or that guy will drill you."

I stepped back and waited. I saw the pitcher wind up. I saw the white ball leave his hand and I swung. I hit nothing.

"Strike one," the ump cried.

Then I swung again. "Strike two."

And I swung again. "Strike three. Game over."

I didn't even get close. And when I got back to Dad he said, "It looked like you were chopping wood out there." Then he kicked the dirt like he was trying to leave a bruise on the planet.

"I tried my best," I said. "I told you I never did it before."

"I'm sorry," he replied. "I'm just a little intense sometimes. I want to win for a change."

"Hey," said Leezy, and I swear I saw her reach out and twisty-pinch Dad on the back of his arm like she was turning his intensity dial down. "Great pitching. An awesome debut. If this were the big leagues you'd already be talked about as the rookie of the year."

I smiled at her and would have just stood there forever with a silly grin on my face, but suddenly the pizza delivery truck pulled up and a guy ran out looking lost. Leezy waved to him. "Over here," she hollered. "You're right on time to feed the next Nolan Ryan."

6

THINKING

When I woke up I wiggled my foot around but Pablo had already crawled out the bottom of the bed and tiptoed out of the room. I left the bedroom door open so he could escape and pee. Yesterday I had kept the door closed and he peed on a pair of Grandma's terry-cloth slippers she had left in the closet. I didn't tell her about the slippers, and when she was at the front door getting another oxygen tank delivery, I stuffed them into the bottom of the kitchen trash then washed my hands.

I rolled out of bed, landed on my feet and hands, and hopped up. I walked over to my dresser. Dad and I now had a system where if he went to work early he'd leave a patch for me in a glass ashtray.

But this morning there was no patch in the ashtray, just a couple of Grandma's cigarette butts, so I knew she had been snooping around my stuff. And I figured Dad must not be up yet.

I pulled on my jeans and went looking for Pablo. When I entered the kitchen Grandma was sucking the air out of her tank so loudly it sounded like someone pumping up a bicycle tire.

"Hello, Sleeping Beauty," she said with a voice that sounded like a board dragged across gravel. "I've been waiting for over two hours for you to get up."

"Is Dad up? He didn't leave me a patch."

"I'm outta cigs," she cackled. "And I'm broke. And your dad's out. Said he had to do some big *thinking*."

"I only have my emergency cash," I said.

"That'll do."

"I don't think I should give it to you," I said. "Not until you tell me where Dad is."

"He's gone," she said. "Everything that man does is a binge and now he's on a *thinking* binge and he's in love with each and every one of his big thoughts. But forget about him for now and *think* about this, mister." She stopped and sucked in a crackling breath. "No cash for me, then no dog for you."

"Pablo!" I shouted, looking left and right and ducking down to peek under the table. "Pablo!" I turned to face Grandma. "Where'd you put him?"

"He's fine," she said. "Five bucks and I'll tell you where he is," she said, and snapped her hand out toward me like a music-box monkey.

"Okay," I agreed. I went into the bedroom and reached into my pillowcase, where I hid the money Mom gave me. I had a twenty-dollar bill and my quarters. When I returned to the kitchen I blurted out, "You can only have five."

"Settle down," she said. "I'll give you change."

I held out the twenty and she snatched it with her quick fingers.

"Where's Pablo?"

"Check the TV cabinet," she said with her voice grinding to a halt as a spasm of coughing left her bent over. She turned and spit something into a matted handkerchief, then leaned back against the counter and closed her eyes.

I ran out to the living room. The TV was tuned to a Sunday church show. I turned down the volume and could hear Pablo whimpering and scratching behind the cabinet door.

I yanked it open and there he was along with the slippers that he had peed in.

"You can't hide a thing from Grandma," she said, inching up on me. "So don't try. If that dog pees on my shoes again I'll put a stamp on his butt and mail him to the Oscar Mayer factory."

"Pablo baby," I cooed, and held him against my chest so that he could look up and lick my chin. His fur smelled as nasty as the slippers.

"Come on," Grandma said. "Enough of this love

fest. You have to get me to the corner store 'cause they won't sell you cigs on account of your age."

"One minute," I said. I got Pablo rinsed off in the kitchen sink and met Grandma on the front porch. The grocery cart with the old couch cushion still in it was on the sidewalk. I helped her climb up the stepladder and got her oxygen tank in place. Then I strapped Pablo in his baby seat and we were off. I went down the street to avoid the broken sidewalk. I wasn't worried about cars because with the way we looked I figured the drivers would be plenty worried about us.

"So," she said, "Have you met Carter's girlfriend yet?"

"Do you mean Leezy?"

"Who else?" she said.

"Yeah."

"I think she's a bad influence on him," she said. "Every time your father gets a girlfriend he forgets he's a born mess, so it doesn't take him long before he loses control of his senses and goes down the drain."

"I thought she was pretty nice," I said. "Every time Dad got crazy at the game she settled him down."

"Well, you haven't seen him unravel like I have," she said. "And I can tell you his downfall always starts with getting a new girlfriend. Just don't tell your mom about her. If you have any hope of getting them back together again, you can't tell her about Leezy. I guarantee you, once Leezy gets wind of how nuts he is she'll head for the hills. You can bet on that!"

I could feel myself being pulled apart between Mom and Dad as I kept pushing the rattling cart down the street. I was wondering if when you got married you always told the other person the truth all the time. Because it seemed to me that I could only tell Mom *some* of the things about Dad, and I could only tell him *some* of the things about her. Then I thought, maybe that's why their marriage broke up, because they couldn't tell the whole truth to each other.

When we got to the store there wasn't a curb ramp, so Grandma said to park her out front.

"Tell the cashier—either Betty or Claire—to come out here and speak to me if they need proof that the cigs aren't for you."

I lifted Pablo and brought him with me. I didn't want her to dog-nap him for the rest of my twenty dollars.

When I asked the cashier for two packs of generic menthols she gave them to me without blinking an eyelash. "They're for my grandma," I explained. "She's outside in a shopping cart."

"Better her than you," she said dryly. Before I could get out of the store I grabbed a can of dog food and a shoe-shaped chew toy for Pablo. He was already up to his old peeing tricks, and I didn't want him chewing too. Next time Grandma might hide him in the freezer. I also got some new batteries for my tape player.

When I returned with the cigarettes Grandma ripped a pack open like they were the only medicine in the world to save her from a rattlesnake bite. She got one started and puffed so much that all the way home I kept thinking we were like an old train.

By the time I made it back to our sidewalk Dad was home and I was half wilted.

"Hey," he hollered from the front porch. "Don't wear yourself out pushing Mom. She can get around just fine if she wants and we got an important game today. If we ace this one we'll be back in second place and breathing down the necks of that bogus O-Men Tire team."

"Then help me get her out of here," I said. "Last time I tried she almost fell over."

Dad reached in and disconnected her hose. Then he picked her up with his arms under her knees and bony back. Suddenly he got a mischievous look on his face and began to spin her around and around in circles until she was dizzy, then he stood her up on the porch and she staggered over to the wall. While he slapped his leg and laughed she moaned and wheezed and inched her way toward the door.

"Hey, Dad," I said, and reached out to steady Grandma before she fell over. "Can I call Mom?"

"Sure," he said, still laughing at what he'd done.

I led Grandma into the house and set her on the couch.

"My oxygen," she begged.

I ran back out to the cart and brought it to her. She smiled and gave my hand a squeeze and I looked down at her and couldn't feel anything else about her except for how sorry I felt that she was in such bad shape.

"You okay?" I asked, as she began to breathe more evenly.

She just nodded. Then between breaths she said, "Mark my words . . . I'm gonna get . . . that son-of-a-gun. He's been sneak-drinkin' again and all I got to do is call your mom and"—she snapped her fingers—"she'll be here in a second."

I turned and ran for the telephone. I wanted to get there first. Mom answered right away and I was so happy to hear her voice I started talking like a switch had been flicked on.

"I pitched in a game and it was great and I have another game today," I blurted out, full of happiness. "I like baseball and I didn't even know it."

"I used to love baseball," she said. "Get your dad to show you the Roberto Clemente ball I gave him a million years ago. It should be worth a bundle by now."

Whoops, I thought. I didn't want to tell her I had

skinned that ball all up so you could hardly find the signature. "I didn't know you liked baseball," I said.

"There are a lot of things about me you don't know," she replied, suddenly sounding like a stranger, as if I had always lived with Dad and she was the one I didn't know.

"Dad likes baseball too," I said. "Maybe you could come down and the three of us could go to a game together."

"Don't go there, Joey," she said with the same cold voice she had used on me in the car. "Ask your dad to show you the scar over his eye where I bounced Roberto Clemente off his thick head."

But I wasn't listening to her. I just had a picture in my mind of Mom, Dad, and me and Pablo at a Pirates baseball game. The four of us in a row, or in a circle, or a square, or standing on top of each other's shoulders like a nutty circus act, all eating those foot-long hot dogs and sharing a bucket of soda. It didn't matter how we were—as long as we were four. "Hey, Dad," I yelled across the room, "do you want to talk with Mom?"

As I waited for his answer I could hear Mom saying, "No. No. Joey, no. Joey, do you hear me?"

I heard her, but I wasn't listening.

"Sure," Dad said. "I'd love to speak with her." As he came toward the phone he passed a mirror and for a moment he paused and ran his hand through his hair as if Mom was at the front door and he was trying to look handsome for her.

I handed him the phone. "Hi, Fran," he said, and then turned away and hunched his shoulders over for some privacy.

"Tell her she can come visit," I said, and circled round to see his face, but he kept circling away from me until the cord had him wrapped up like Houdini.

"Tell her to visit!" I yelled, and danced from foot to foot. "Visit! Visit!"

He turned to me and snapped angrily, "Stop it. She doesn't want to visit."

"Make her," I said. "Tell her you want her to come."

Dad jammed his finger in his free ear as he listened, and spoke. "Yeah, I've been keeping up with his medicine. Yeah, I think he's changed it today. Yeah, I know it's important. Yeah, I'm living up to my responsibilities. No, I don't think I need your advice. Yeah, here's Joey."

He handed me the phone like it was something smelly.

"Have you been changing your patch?" she asked.

"Yeah," I said. "Well—not today yet."

"You sound just like your dad," she said.

"We're guys," I replied. "This is how guys sound."

I glanced over at Dad. He winked at me and I

winked back. "Hey, Dad," I yelled so Mom could hear over the phone, "when can we go back to the tattoo parlor?"

Dad's eyes bugged out and he put his finger over his lips.

"Joey," Mom said, "listen to me. I want you to hang up this phone and immediately change your patch. You got that? Or do I have to come get you?"

"I got it," I said miserably, knowing I had gone too far. "I was just joking."

"How come I'm not laughing?" she said. "You know why? Because you scare me when you get carried away and I'm not around to know if you are joking or gyrating. You know what I mean?"

"I know," I said, while suddenly wanting to get off the phone as desperately as I had a few minutes ago wanted to get on it. "I'll let you know how the game goes," I said.

"Yeah," she said. "Do an official score sheet and mail it to me. I like stats."

As soon as I put down the phone Dad had his hand on my shoulder. "Come on," he said. "You seem fine to me, but we better get that patch changed before your mom shows up with a lawyer."

"Hey, Dad," I asked, "let me see the scar over your eye."

He squatted down and pointed to a red line that looked like a tiny railroad track. "This is where she beaned me," he said. "And now that I think of it, I bet you got your good arm from her."

As soon as we were in the car Dad started talking. It was like he couldn't stand to have anything moving faster than his mouth. "You know, Joey, all morning I been over at Storybook Land," Dad said as he lit up a cigarette. "I went over to see ol' Humpty Dumpty and do some solid *thinking*. Humpty didn't let me down. Here's what I came up with. In life you gotta have a goal. Big ones or small ones, I don't care what size. Just have a goal and right now we have the same goal—Joey, I know you want to know me better and I want to know you better. This is the whole reason why you are here this summer. But, we can't share my past. And when you leave here and return to your mom, I won't be there to share your future. But right now—this summer—you and me—this is the time for us. We can win this baseball championship and long after you are gone I can think of this time and how my boy and me were the biggest winners on the field. This is our goal, Joey—to be champions together. This is what I've been thinking about all morning. And who knows, maybe next year you can come back and we can do it all over again. But one thing at a time. Let's be winners now. What do you say?"

I just looked over at him and I had tears in my eyes because it was something I wanted to hear in the worst way. And as I stared at him he reached out and put his hand on mine and I could feel it shaking and before long mine began to shake too.

"Let's do it," I said. "Let's be the champs."

"Right on," he said.

"But I'm gonna need help," I said. "I really don't know what I'm doing."

"Don't sweat it," he said. "Remember, you are the caveman with the rock. That's all you need to know. Now listen to this. Leezy and I were working on the lineup and we both decided you were our number-one pitcher. We were talking strategy. First we gotta beat Ritter's Diner tonight. Then we gotta beat Emerson Real Estate, then take the semifinals, then knock off whoever is in the other PAL field for the North Side Championship."

"Do I have to pitch every game?" I asked.

"Yeah, Joey," he said. "Otherwise we don't stand a chance. But I'm excusing you from practices. I don't want you wearing out your arm."

"Hey, Dad," I said, "can you make sure Grandma and Pablo come to the game and that Pablo wears his jersey? He's my good-luck charm."

"Will it make you pitch better?" Dad asked.

"Yeah," I said.

"No problem," he promised. "When you take the mound they'll be in the stands. Scout's honor. I'll have Leezy get them."

I smiled. I wanted Pablo to watch me win.

7

MY GAME

The good feeling between Dad and me didn't last much beyond the first inning. As soon as the game against Ritter's Diner started it went in two directions at once. There was my game, and there was Dad's game. My game was calm, his was not. First, like Dad said, the caveman with the rock rules. And I had the rock. I know I told Mom I liked baseball, but not all of it. I only liked the pitching part, which to me was still like throwing rocks at targets in the back yard, except with a baseball game there were a lot of other people standing around staring at me, which I didn't like because all those eyes made me itchy and nervous.

I loved being on the mound. I thought of it as a giant patch under my feet. As long as I was standing on it I was fine. But when I stepped off, the whole world would spin around like a top.

That's why I never covered first on a grounder to the first baseman because it meant leaving the mound. I didn't want to do it, so I didn't do it, even when Dad yelled out, "Don't make me come onto the field and drag you over there next time!" I knew he wasn't going to come out to the mound. He had been out twice before to yell at me for not listening to him and the ump told him if he came out a third time he'd have to change pitchers. So he just stood by the dugout and hollered at me, but I didn't even look at him. Between batters I just strolled toe-to-heel around the edge of my mound like a tightrope walker. And if a batter happened to get a hit, then I just struck out the next batter. I also refused to back up the catcher on a throw to the plate even when Dad ordered me to do it. "You have to do it!" he commanded. "I'm your coach. I'm your father!" I just turned my back on him and stared off into the outfield while everyone ran around chasing the ball, or trying to stay away from it. I didn't catch infield pop-ups even when Dad pointed up into the air at them from the coach's box and called out that it was mine to catch. If I couldn't reach it from the mound, I let it drop or someone else had to catch it. And I didn't field bunts either. I just stood my ground and threw the *rock*. That's all I did, which was enough. I left everything else for the other guys to do.

By about the fourth inning Dad had gone ballistic, which by then I understood was easy to make him do.

The more he yelled the less I did, and the more he lost control.

"Joey," he hollered with his hands cupped around his mouth after I let a pop-fly bunt drop about an inch outside the mound and a run scored from third. "Please, son. If you are mad at me just say so. Don't blow the game. We can talk about why you're mad at me later. But for the love of Pete please pick up the bunts before the whole darn team figures out they can *bunt* their way to victory."

I wasn't worried about their bunting. I just rolled my head around like my neck was tight and kept my mouth shut. The mound was a good place for me to *think* and I guess I was silent with Dad to pay him back for all the times I'd hoped he would come and talk to me but never did. So I was just giving him a taste of his own medicine. Then, as he flew into the middle of another yelling spree, I'd strike out the next batter and make him smile and holler things like, "You're the man!"

But after three outs I had to leave the mound and go to the dugout, which I dreaded. I left the ball on the rubber for the next pitcher and then pulled my hat all the way down over my face like it was a Halloween mask, and peeked out the little air-vent holes. I wished the other team had all their twenty-seven outs in a row. Because when I got off I had to listen nonstop to Dad, but worse, I had to bat, and I hated to bat more than anything I ever did in my life. I didn't like people throwing rocks at me because really, it reminded me of the times when I used to run like a crazy rabbit all the way home from school with kids chasing me and throwing real rocks at me which sometimes hit me and hurt. Every time I stood at the plate and watched the pitcher wind up, I could feel every muscle in my body getting stiff and contorted and so when I took a swing I closed my eyes and looked like I was hacking at a piñata. And it was the laughs and boos of the other players along with Dad's constant jawing that bothered me most. I just wanted to hit the ball to shut everyone up, but I couldn't get near it, and all the way back to the dugout with my chin down and the bat dragging a line in the clay I could hear those words hurled at me like stones.

"Whiff king!"

"Pansy bat!"

"Turnstile!"

I wanted us to score a lot of runs and win the game but I was always happy when our team got its third out and I could go back to the mound and do only what I was good at, which was throw hard at the catcher's glove and let the rest of the team do everything else.

We beat Ritter's Diner seven to three. It was easy.

And I could tell that the people who saw the game knew what Dad knew, that I was an awesome caveman with a rock.

The moment I struck out the last batter Dad got all happy again and stopped being so intense, which made me happy too. "That's my boy out there!" he yelled to everyone in the stands. "He's the pride of the Pigzas!" Even Grandma stood and held Pablo up to her chest and he was yapping and paddling his arms and legs with happiness just as Dad was. I stood on the mound and wished that moment would never end. But it did. People stopped cheering and started walking toward their cars and I put the ball on the rubber and headed for the dugout.

Instead of going home Leezy invited us to the store. She and Grandma and Pablo went to pick up a pizza. On the way over Dad kept talking and talking about how I crushed them, stomped them, and atomized them. I looked over at his mouth, which never seemed to close—not even the lips touched together—and it made me dizzy to listen to him, and I cringed when he said he'd been "*thinking* again."

"Your coming to visit has been the greatest gift to me," he said. "You make me feel like a winner. That is the best thing that has ever happened to me except now I feel so darn *guilty*." He hung his head. "I've been an awful dad and here you are a great kid and I sure would feel a lot better if I could give you something so great it would make up for *everything*."

I was going to tell him that it wasn't important to make up for everything. That what we were doing right now was fine with me, but before I could get my thoughts into words he suddenly swerved sharply and stopped in front of a little store. "Be right back," he said, and left the engine running.

As soon as he was out of sight I slid over to the driver's seat. I held the steering wheel. I reached forward and touched the gas pedal with my toe. The engine roared. I pressed the brake.

I was adding up how many years it would be before I got my license when Dad jumped into the passenger side with a bag of ice. "Put it in gear, big man, and take me to the mall."

"Are you joking?" I asked.

"Half," he said. "But give it a try. If you mess up I'll just reach over and grab the wheel."

Maybe this is what happens when you become a winner, I thought. You get to do really good stuff. I put my foot on the brake and pushed the gearshift into reverse and when I lifted my foot we rolled out into the street.

"Put it in drive," Dad said.

I did. Then I straightened out the wheel and pressed on the gas, but I was so short that when I slouched down to press the gas I couldn't see over the dashboard. Then I felt Dad grab the steering wheel.

"You work the pedals," he said, "I'll work the wheel." And we did that all the way into the parking lot.

"Can I get a car?" I asked.

"Sure," he said. "I started driving when I was your age. My dad had a farm and I used to drive the tractor everywhere."

That made me happy and all I could think about was me behind the wheel of a car, zipping all over the place with Pablo sitting up on the dashboard like some kind of yapping dog horn.

As soon as we got to the mall I wanted to run around and do all the kid stuff. "Can I have fifty cents?" I asked Dad. "I want to ride the bucking bronco."

He dug into his pocket and pulled out a dime. "Go over to the wishing well," he said, pointing to a little fountain. "See if there are some quarters in there."

"I can't do that," I said. "It's stealing."

"No it's not," he replied. "The janitor just takes it anyway. Now go get some quarters."

"I can't," I said.

"Then skip it," he said. "Let's get to the store so I can ice your arm down. We don't want any swelling. You got to pitch in a few days, but don't worry. A kid with your talent can pitch every three days, no problem."

"Can I have a Coke?" I asked. "I'm thirsty."

"Leezy and Grandma and Pablo will be here any minute," he said. "She's bringing pop."

When we arrived at the store Dad waved to the man at the cash register. "Hello, Jake. We're going to the back room to ice down this rocket."

Jake looked at me and smiled. "Already heard about you, young fellow. Gonna make Steel City Sports a winner."

"Hope so," I replied, then followed Dad to Leezy's office, where he found an old T-shirt that he stuffed with ice and taped around my arm.

I was really happy when Leezy, Pablo, and Grandma arrived because Dad was just talking a mile a minute while my arm froze and cold drops of water dripped from my fingertips onto the carpet.

"What an arm," Leezy said. "You were fabulous." Then she opened a small refrigerator and pulled out two beers. She twisted the top off one for Dad and one for herself. "To the hope of Steel City Sports," she said, clinking bottles with Dad.

Dad put the bottle to his lips and tilted the bottom up for a moment and when he set it down it was empty. And in an instant he had his hand wrapped around another. "That first one was so lonely, it needs a friend to keep it company," he said, smiling.

"Dad," I started, but before I could say anything else he read my mind and started talking.

"It's beer," he replied, and held the bottle up for me to see. "Drinking beer is not like drinking whiskey or vodka. It's beer. You know, soda pop for grownups."

I didn't know what to say so I smiled at him and said the goofiest thing that came into my mind. "Can I have a beer too?" I asked.

"No," he blurted out with so much force a little beer foam leaked out the corner of his mouth and he wiped it off on his wrist. "Absolutely not. Where did you get that idea?"

Grandma was opening the pizza and sliding slices onto paper plates. "He didn't get it from me," she said. "Remember, Carter, I didn't let you drink until you made the junior varsity baseball team."

I looked down at Pablo. "Pablo might like a beer," I suggested.

"Well, he'll get one long before you. As soon as Pablo is three dog years old he'll be twenty-one human years and he can drink an ocean of beer if he wants. But not until then."

Still, even though we were joking around, I knew beer was bad and he shouldn't be drinking it.

Dad stopped talking long enough to glance over at Leezy, who was staring at him like something was wrong.

"I'd better go check on how Jake's doing," she said, putting her unfinished beer on her desk. "I gotta close out the register and lock up."

As soon as she left Dad reached for her beer and just as quickly finished it.

"Dad," I said again, but couldn't get the rest of the words out before he talked right over me.

"There's no reason to get excited and tell you-know-who because you know how she can get. And we don't want her getting all worked up and ruining our father-son fun just because of a little beer."

I wasn't thinking about how she can get. I was wondering how he could get. Mom had always told me that he went from a lamb to a lion in no time flat once he had a drink. And as I looked at him change in front of my eyes I started thinking about myself, because it was like my patch had disappeared and I was suddenly back to my old wired Joey again.

As soon as he went to the toilet Grandma said, "Remember what I told you. As soon as he gets a new girlfriend he thinks he can handle a drink. But mark my words, he can't. If you think he's bad to talk now, wait until he has a few under his belt and I promise you you'll tape your ears shut. God only knows why I put up with it. I guess it's always the same for a mom. Yours puts up with you because you are her son, and I put up with him for the same reason."

When Dad came out of the bathroom he suddenly looked at his watch. "We better get going," he said.

"I'm tired," I replied. I unwrapped the tape from around the T-shirt and shook the ice out in the trash can. Then I lifted Pablo off the seat of his chair where he had been eating little round slices of pepperoni I had set aside for him. "I want to go to bed," I announced. I said good night to Leezy on my way out to the car and fell asleep to the sound of Dad's voice as he drove home.

8

THE GIFT

I didn't know what time it was when Dad woke me up. It was dark out and everything seemed quiet, like it was the middle of the night.

"Did you brush your teeth before bed?" he asked, and I could smell the beer on his breath.

"No," I said.

"Well, get up and come to the bathroom. Your mom would kill me if I didn't make you brush your teeth," he said.

I washed my face and the moment I stuck the toothbrush in my mouth he started talking. "I been *thinkin'*," he said.

Even though I was sleepy I knew his thinkin' was somehow going to be worse for me than for him.

"I know I wasn't there for you for your whole life," he started. "And I been struggling with how to make it up to you. Like what would be the greatest gift I could give you? And then just now, bingo! I was on the front porch and it came to me. I've been thinkin' about these patches," he said, holding the box of them in his hand. "I bet if you didn't wear them you'd never know the difference."

I spit into the sink. "You'd know the difference," I said. "And so would I."

"I've always found," he said, sitting down on the lowered toilet seat, "that if I need to lick a problem I just tackle it cold turkey. Take my alcohol problem, for example—the last time I was arrested for DWI the judge threw me in jail and there was no booze there. None. Believe me, they didn't give me a little old alcohol patch. Nope. It was just me and the walls and, buddy, they sent me to a work farm and in the beginning I thought I'd go bonkers. But day by day I got better. I worked like a demon under the sun in those fields, and the old poison just sweat out of me until I got a grip on myself and beat it. It was *force of will*!" He gave out a low whistle and made a muscle, then slapped it with his hand. "The mind is a muscle," he said as he pointed to his head, "and determination is the exercise that keeps it tough!"

"But that was alcohol," I said. "Mine is real medicine. A doctor gave it to me."

"Same difference," he said, and smirked. "A bartender gave me mine."

"Well, what about your nicotine patch?" I shot back, and pointed to his shoulder with the yellow-eyed skull tattoo.

"You got me there," he said, and for a moment I thought all his big ideas would pass and he'd agree with me and go to bed.

But then he said, "Look at me. I'm a hypocrite. 'Do as I say, don't do as I do.' No kid would listen to a dad who is that way. I'm telling you to suck it up while I use this crutch. Well, no more." He reached across his body and peeled the flesh-colored patch off his shoulder. "No more drugs," he growled. He balled it up in his hands and tossed it into the toilet.

"My patch is not a drug," I pleaded. "It's medicine."

"It's a drug," Dad insisted, and reached for me. "It's a crutch."

I stepped away. "It's a help," I replied. "I have to wear it. You don't know what happens to me when I don't have it."

"What could happen to you? You'd find out that you are okay. Is that it? You'd find out that you aren't some drug-dependent guinea pig for doctors? Joey, son," he said, "the greatest thing I could do for you is to show you that you are a normal kid and don't need this stuff."

"I'm already a normal kid," I said.

"Not with that patch on," he said, reaching toward me again. "Normal kids don't need medicine every day."

I just stood there with my back to the wall and lowered my head because I knew what was coming and there was nothing I could do about it.

"I watched you pitch out there today and I don't think there is a thing wrong with you. Nothing. I don't think you need that medicine. Heck, giving you medicine is like giving a fish more water."

I wanted him to stop telling me who I was when I knew better. He wanted me to be something I wasn't, and I wanted him to be something he wasn't. We were so far apart. And yet, even though I knew he was wrong, he was my dad, and I wanted him to be right. More than anything, I wanted him to have all the answers.

Then he reached under my shirt quick as a cat and ripped off my patch. "You are liberated," he announced seriously. "You are your own man, in control of your own life—and free as a bird." He held the patch between his fingers like it was a crusty scab and dropped it in the toilet. "No more patches," he said. "You don't need them. You're going to be a winner without them."

"I don't think so," I whispered.

"There's no going back now," he said. "We don't need this stuff. Real men can tough it out. Be determined. Don't you tell your mom," he said. "She'll be upset with me. But once you show her you don't need this stuff, she'll really respect what I'm doing here."

Then he stood up and lifted the lid of the toilet. And one by one he took my patches out of the box and balled them up in his fist and dropped them into the bowl. I tried to reach for them but he held me back with one hand.

"You're in my house now, buddy. You may not know it yet but the greatest gift I can give you is to take something away from you. Funny, isn't it?"

It wasn't funny to me. Especially when he flushed the tank and kept flushing it over and over as he dropped the patches into the swirling water, and as they spun around in that funnel I felt it was me who was spinning around and around and being flushed down a hole. I just started to cry. I didn't jump around and bang my head on things or bounce off the walls or pitch a fit in any way. I just stood still and quietly cried. And I was thinking to myself, The next time you cry you won't be standing still. You'll be dancing a little crazy jig like a person being stung by a million bees. I remembered how that felt.

I looked at myself in the mirror and I still had toothpaste in my mouth and around my lips and already I looked like a mad dog.

"Now be a good boy and finish brushing," Dad said once the last patch had disappeared. "Your mom will kill me if you get a cavity while I'm looking out for you."

I brushed a little more, then said good night and

trudged back to my bedroom. I crawled into bed and pulled Pablo up and tucked him between my shoulder and chin. I kissed him on the head and felt his whiskers tickle my lips. I kept thinking that there must be some way for me to talk Dad into changing his mind. Even though I knew the patches were down the drain, maybe we could get new ones. Maybe he could tell Mom he lost them. She'd be mad but she'd get more for me.

I wanted to get up and call her. But I could hear him crossing the living room. The refrigerator door opened and bottles rattled and clinked. A bottle hissed as its cap was twisted off, and Dad plopped back down on the sofa to watch TV.

"You shouldn't be drinking," I heard Grandma say. "Go to bed."

"It's just beer," he replied. "If you don't like it, you can pack your oxygen tank and hit the road."

She didn't say anything more and I lay in bed and all I could imagine was the worst part of me getting on a train a long ways off. That old Joey was coming to get me and I couldn't do anything about it. Day by day he would get closer. Even if I got up and started running away, he would catch me. There was nothing to do but wait, and worry. And worry wouldn't protect me, so I closed my eyes and told myself to sleep while I could.

9

DOWNTOWN

I opened one eye like it was a periscope going up and scanning the room for safety. I looked left, then right. I didn't see Dad, and Pablo was up and gone. Grandma must have opened the bedroom door and let him out. I slid out of bed and tiptoed over to my dresser. I checked the ashtray for a patch. It was empty. I put my hand in anyway and ran my finger around the inside like I was trying to get the last drop out of a bowl of soup.

"Okay," I whispered to myself. "Take a deep breath, and like Mom told you, if you want to make good choices, think one thought at a time."

First thought: I figured I could call Mom and tell her right away to come get me, and then I could listen to her tell me "I told you he was no good" all the way home and I'd never have another chance with Dad again.

Second thought: I could stick with Dad and find out that I was normal without the medicine. I wanted to believe what he said. I wanted to believe that I was like any other kid.

Third thought: I remembered how I had been without my good meds in the past.

Fourth thought: I wanted to give myself another chance.

I peeked my head around the edge of the doorjamb and saw Grandma leaning against the kitchen counter with the oxygen tank between her ankles. She was knitting something like a scarf for a giraffe. "I didn't sleep too well," she said to Dad, who was staring into the refrigerator. "I been up all night with the nervous worries. Your drinkin' again's not right."

"Well, I slept like a baby," he said, and stretched his arms like a cat. "If you didn't worry so much you would too." He was showered and shaved and from across the room I could smell his cinnamon chewing gum. "Hey, buddy," he said, spotting me when he turned around. "I've been waiting for you. Hurry up. There's nothing in the fridge. We'll eat breakfast downtown and you can see the sights while I punch the clock."

"Yeah," I said. "I'd like that."

"Brush your teeth," he said, and pointed to the

bathroom, which reminded me of the night before. I nodded and went into the little room and closed the door and waited to bounce around the walls like a cricket trapped in a shoe box, but nothing like that happened. I just squeezed a perfect line of paste on my brush and brushed my teeth like any normal kid. I washed my face and combed my hair over to cover my bald spot. When I returned to my room and got dressed the thought of being able to walk around Pittsburgh as a totally normal drug-free kid was pretty exciting. I felt like I was a caged animal being released back into the wild. I put my tape player in my pocket, and my trumpet in my backpack along with the money I pulled out of my pillowcase. I heard Dad start the car and I ran, dodging through the maze of furniture in the living room. "Goodbye," I yelled to Grandma and to Pablo, who was busy chewing a hole in a couch cushion. Normally I would pull him out and scold him, but I was late so I let it go. He and Grandma can work that one out without me, I thought.

"You want to drive?" Dad asked when I opened the car door. "Practice makes perfect."

"Not today," I said, thinking that it might be dangerous. If I lost control of myself downtown who knows how many people would have tire tracks down their backs.

As soon as I slammed my door it was like a starter's

pistol had fired and Dad's mouth was off and running. "You know, Joey, I woke up thinkin' about how last night was a turning point in my life. With a couple of flushes of the toilet, I really got a load off my chest. And just like that," he snapped his fingers, "you and I are even. All that old guilt is gone and I'm ready to move forward. I feel like a new man. How about you?"

I wanted to say that last night was a turning point in my life too, but I wasn't sure just yet what direction it was going to turn.

"I don't know if I feel like a new man or my old self," I said. "I just don't know, but I'm hoping for the best."

"Don't worry," he said, "by the end of the day you'll see your dad was right again. You gotta have faith in me, pal." He stuck out his hand. "Give me five," he said.

I slapped mine down on his hard enough to leave a blood blister. Then I held mine out. He swung his open hand down and I pulled mine away. He toppled forward and the car swerved to one side.

"Aren't you ever going to catch on to that?" I asked as I helped him back up.

"I better before it kills me," he replied, and steered the car back between the lines. Then, once it was clear to me that he was still in a good mood and wouldn't bite my nose off, I said, "You scared me by drinking last night."

"That shouldn't scare you," Dad replied. "I do my

best thinkin' after a little drinkin', and look at me today. I'm as good as new. And look at you. No patch, and you're on top of the world."

"But I thought you told Mom you quit drinking, because she told me to call her if you drink and now it scares me not to call her."

"To be totally honest," Dad said, "your mom would like you to have a dad who didn't act like a man. Don't get me wrong, she's a wonderful woman, but when it comes to men she thinks we should do everything by her girl rules. But we're men, Joey. We have our own way of doing things, and especially our own way of solving some of life's bigger problems. Like I said last night, we just pull ourselves up by the bootstraps and move on. We don't talk about our problems every single hour of every single day. Know what I mean? Plus, your mom would baby you along on medicine for the rest of your life. To *me* that is not a solution. Now, you can call your mom if you want. But I think you should be a man, and prove to everyone that you don't have any problems you can't fix yourself."

"Is all that true?" I asked.

"Of course it's true," he said. "Man to man. You can't go out into the world for five minutes without a woman telling you what to do. Mark my words."

When we got to the diner, Dad didn't even ask me what I wanted. "Two Hungry Man specials," he called out to the waitress as we took our seats, "with extra sides." When the food arrived, there was a ton of sausage and bacon and toast with melted butter and silver dollar pancakes and fried eggs and we chowed down and it was a good feeling to be hungry, and a better feeling as my belly got full as a new moon.

"How're you making out?" he asked, and wiped a folded slice of toast across his slick plate.

"Great. I'm not hyper one bit," I said, as I peeled back the sticky tops on all the little jelly tubs and started to suck the warm jelly out.

"I mean your arm," he replied. "I'm tired of talking about problems. That's women's talk. Now eat up, you got to build strength for the next game."

I waved my hand for the waitress. "Excuse me. Could I have some more strawberry jelly, please?"

"Are you sure this much jelly is good for you?" she asked, and pointed her pen at the empty tubs.

I didn't know what to say, so I smiled real big and she gave me some apple jelly because nobody eats that tasteless stuff. People don't even take it home with them unless they want to use it for glue.

As soon as the waitress turned away Dad leaned toward me. "See what I mean about women always butting in?" he said. "What should she care if you eat a *bathtub* full of jelly? Okay, while we're talking about men stuff, I put together a big new *guy* plan for us. Now that I got you off the drugs, you might decide you're better off living with me. We'll keep doing the

Police Athletic League circuit until you go to high school. By then you'll be a prospect and colleges will recruit you. Then you can go to Pitt here in town and pitch for the Panthers. I'll become your agent and get you drafted into the minor leagues, where you'll only spend a short while until a big league team calls you up. Then bingo—you'll be an *awesome force*. What do you think?"

"What will Mom think?" I asked.

"I'll handle that part," he said, waving his fork across his face. "What do you think?"

"You know I can't help you get back together with Mom if you drink," I said.

"I have news for you, Joey. I don't want to get back together with your mom. That's over with. She's not the right woman for me anyway," he replied.

"Does that mean Leezy is the right woman because she lets you drink?"

"There's more to it than that," he said. "But she and I talked about getting a place together. And I'm sure she'd like it if you were there. Hey, already she likes you better than me. Really, she can't stop talking about you. So what do you think?"

I didn't know what more to think, so I just blurted out what I say when I don't have an answer. "Can I get back to you on that?" I said. "It's a big step."

"Speaking of steps," he declared, suddenly looking at his watch. "Let's beat feet. People on the bottom of the food chain can't be late." He threw some money on the counter, stuffed a five-dollar bill in my shirt pocket, and hopped up. I followed him out the door.

"See that building over there?" He pointed toward something that looked like a Greek temple. "That's the War Memorial. I'll meet you there at four. If you need me earlier I'll be upstairs setting up chairs in the conference room." Then he started walking quickly in that direction.

"Thanks for breakfast!" I yelled, and stuck out my belly and jiggled it like I was a sumo wrestler.

He whipped around and pointed into the air. "Hey, don't be a Chicken Little today. The sky isn't falling. Have fun." Then he turned and walked off.

I looked up into the air. The sky was solid blue. Not a crack in sight. "You better stay put," I whispered. "I'm taking a big chance on me and I need this to work."

When I realized I was speaking to the sky I closed my mouth and looked around. A woman waiting for a bus was staring at me. "I'm not taking drugs anymore," I said. She smiled, and turned away.

I wasn't sure what to visit first, so I decided to play a game that was always good for getting things started. I stood in place by the bus stop and spun around in circles, faster and faster, with my finger pointing straight out like I was the spinner on a game board of downtown Pittsburgh. When I screeched to a stop I opened my eyes and followed my finger down the road.

I hadn't gone all that far when I saw a video game arcade. Okay, Joey Pigza, I said to myself, if you are going to lose it, this is the place that will send you around the bend. I went inside and changed half of the five dollars Dad gave me into tokens and took a seat in the race car booth. I thought I would practice my high-speed driving before Dad put me behind the wheel again. I slipped the money in, gripped the wheel, and pressed on the gas. My car peeled out and instantly I started whizzing around a track with a dozen other Indy cars. We smashed into each other. I spun out and hit a wall. I ran off the road into the bales of hay. I scattered the mechanics as I roared through my pit. Finally, I ran out of time and my car slowed down. YOU ARE OUT OF FUEL read the screen. I put more money in and pressed the gas. I didn't care if I won the race or not. It was fun just to swerve like a maniac all over the track and have the other drivers shake their fists at me as I sideswiped them. After I forced one car into the stands, it burst into a ball of flame and sent the fans screaming for the exit. For a moment I wondered if I was the one who was out of control. "Relax, it's just a game," I said to myself. By then I was out of tokens, so I hopped up and walked outside. I must be doing okay, I thought. Usually when I'm in an arcade I'm running from machine to machine and playing everything until I'm totally broke and then I look all over the floor for dropped money, and check the coin returns, and tip machines forward to look under them, and pester the arcade attendant for free tokens until he flips me a few and when I ask for a few more he boots me out because it is obvious that I'm an out-of-control pest.

But I didn't go manic and spend everything. I had my fun. I spent my limit. And I walked away with total self-control. Maybe Dad is right, I thought. I don't need the patch. I just need to act like a man.

I was so excited about feeling good I wanted to call Mom. Most of the pay phones were on outside street corners and the car horns were louder than my trumpet, so I went into a department store and found a phone booth by the snack bar. I put in a quarter from Mom's phone money and dialed her number. The operator came on and told me to deposit "three dollars for the first three minutes." I did, but the telephone rang and rang until after I counted twenty rings I figured she wasn't there unless she was in the shower, so I let it ring twenty more times. I hung up, got all my quarters back, and then I called the beauty parlor.

"Beauty and the Beast," Tiffany, the receptionist, answered. "Can I help you?"

"It's me, Joey," I said. "Is my mom there?"

"She's on vacation," Tiffany replied. "Said she needed a few days to herself."

"Where'd she go?" I asked, and I could feel my chest getting tight.

"Didn't say. Maybe Mexico."

"Mexico? She doesn't know anyone in Mexico. She doesn't even like Mexican food. Why'd she go there?"

"It's just a guess, Joey. Now hold for a minute," she said, "I've got another call."

Mexico? I thought. Why there? Why didn't she tell me? And I could feel myself getting all twisted up inside like when bad things *do* happen. Maybe Dad told her I wanted to stay with him and instead of getting mad she decided to run off and celebrate. Suddenly the operator came on and told me to put more money in the phone so I just hung up and told myself to calm down. Maybe Mom went down to Mexico to get me another Chihuahua as a surprise for me when I came home. Maybe she went to Tijuana to hear Herb Alpert. There were many good reasons to go to Mexico. And as Mom always told me, when you feel mixed up always try to think positive thoughts.

So I ran outside and cupped my hands around my mouth and faced what I thought was Mexico and I yelled out at the top of my lungs, "Have a great time south of the border and bring me back something good!" That made me feel much better, except I had to go to the bathroom so I ran back inside the store.

I was cutting through the boys' clothing section when I passed a kid that looked like somebody I knew from school. I turned to say hello to him, but realized he wasn't a real kid at all but a mannequin. Then I started examining the mannequin. It was the most real-looking one I had ever seen, and the kid seemed perfect in every way. The hair was just the right blond and the right length. Very cool sunglasses covered his eyes, which were blue and bright. The nose was medium size and straight. The lips were barely open, as if he were going to say something perfectly polite. The chin was strong. His skin was as smooth as new vinyl, with no bumps, scars, moles, weird hairs, or pimples. Not even freckles. His arms were reaching out as if he were going to catch a beach ball. His bathing suit and T-shirt were new and clean and he was wearing sandals. Even his feet were perfect.

I just kept staring at him. There he is, I thought, the perfect kid, and I bet he is perfectly *normal* too. I wondered how it would feel to be one-hundred-percent flawless in every way so that from waking up in the morning to going to sleep at night I didn't make one mistake, big or small. Like, I didn't even get itsy-bitsy crumbs on the floor, or feel moody, or forget to feed Pablo. Maybe the store could sell perfect kids that could be placed like mannequins around the house, just sitting next to their toy boxes without ever making a mess, or taking fake showers without ever getting a huge puddle of water on the floor. Or you could put them out in the front yard like garden statues waving to the neighbors or holding a goofy flag with a bright flower on it. Mom once said it was my mistakes that made me interesting, and although I didn't understand her then, I did now.

Then I got a great idea. I went to the clothes rack and got a beach outfit and went into the bathroom and put it on. I hid all my stuff in my backpack, then dashed over to the mannequin. I hopped up and stood on the fake painted beach like I was his friend and took his sunglasses off and fit them on my face. I clipped my tape player to my waistband, pressed in my mini-speakers, and struck a pose like a lifeguard looking out at the surfers. As people walked by they didn't notice me or my new friend.

But I was looking at them. Most everyone was going somewhere in a hurry. And it got to be no fun standing there with no one looking at me, so then I tried to get their attention.

I leaned way forward and stuck out my tongue until my mouth started to ache. People just walked by as if it was nothing. I crossed my eyes and drooled so much it dripped off my chin. Nothing. I did fake hiccups. Nothing. Nobody seemed to notice, because no matter how weird I was, they were just as weird. People argued and picked their noses and swatted their kids and talked to themselves and pulled at their tight underwear and spit chewing gum out in the corners and wiped their dirty hands on the clothes and sang off key and did all kinds of strange things that I did too, which made me feel like I was normal like they were and not perfect like my mannequin buddy.

Finally, a lady who looked like any kid's mom checked the price on my shorts and I began to laugh because it tickled and the woman nearly fainted and then started laughing because what I was doing was funny and she knew it, and I figured she must be nice because most people would pitch a fit.

"What are you doing?" she asked. "Spying for shoplifters?"

"No, I'm just being a mannequin."

"I've always wanted to do something like that," she said. "I just didn't have the nerve."

"The only thing you have to worry about," I whispered, "is that someone will yell at you. But if you are somebody like me, then having someone yell at you is no big deal."

"Well, you better take your place again," she said. "You don't want the clerk to spot you."

"I'm finished," I said, stepping down. "Time to move on. Today is my day to see if I can be normal and have fun all at the same time."

She gave me a strange look when I said "normal," like the last thing in the world I was was "normal." Oh well, I thought, maybe it's not a good idea to be too normal. It didn't sound like much fun if it only made you afraid to do the stuff you really wanted to do.

After I got dressed I went out to the sidewalk, pointed my finger straight out, and spun around with my eyes closed while I sang, "Round and round and round I go, where I stop nobody knows." When I did stop I was pointing at an ice cream parlor across the street. "My lucky day," I said to no one in particular.

While I crossed the street I figured out a little experiment to try. In my mind I picked out the two flavors I would most want on my ice cream cone—chocolate mint and Oreo. But when I went to order I said to the girl, "Give me two scoops of your two most normal flavors."

"What if you don't like them?" she asked.

"I'll spit them out," I replied. "I'm not really hungry for ice cream, this is just a test."

She made me pay in advance. Then she gave me a scoop of vanilla and a scoop of chocolate. "These are our two best-selling flavors," she said, handing the cone to me.

"Are you kidding?" I asked.

"No," she said, "the plain flavors are the most popular."

Well, I thought as I left, I'm not plain either.

When I finished my ice cream I closed my eyes and spun around and around and wondered where I'd land next.

When I stopped and opened my eyes I was pointing at a church with bright red doors. I hadn't been in a church since Grandma took me when I was little. I had filled my pockets with marbles and during the sermon they got loose under the pews. They made a loud racket, but nobody laughed like I did. After that, Grandma made me stay home with her to watch church on TV.

I opened the huge red door and quietly tiptoed up the aisle. The chapel walls were glowing with tall blue-and-red glass windows, and as I walked down the aisle I imagined the dusty shafts of red air and blue air and purple air filling me up inside. And when I breathed out, the same colors swirled around my head. A choir was practicing in the balcony and I took a seat and listened.

"No, no, no!" the conductor shouted. "Tenors, follow the organ. You're flat. Now, again."

The organ started up so loudly I could feel it buzzing in my feet. The tenors sang and the conductor pointed to another group of singers and they came in. "Stop!" he shouted. "You're late, altos. Come in crisply after the first measure. Now, again."

The organ started, the tenors began, and the altos came in on the correct beat, then a third group, which sang even higher, joined in.

"Stop!" shouted the conductor. "Sopranos, take the gum balls out of your mouths. Enunciate! Again."

They started up, but soon the conductor lowered his arms. "Stop. Basses, you've got to hold the bottom. Don't let the tenors pull you into their octave. Again!"

The conductor continued to start and stop and start and stop the singers and it made me nervous and I began to get a funny idea running through me. I wanted to play my trumpet. I reached down into my backpack and slowly pulled it out and set it on my lap. I looked at it. I touched it. I licked my lips. I listened to the choir music which was smooth and creamy as yellow icing on a cake and I was aching to stand up and blow the opening notes to "A Taste of Honey."

Finally the conductor started them from the beginning. It was amazing to listen to them sing one perfect wave of notes on top of another. The more perfectly they sang the more I wanted to join in. I felt as if I were being tickled all over but wasn't allowed to laugh. All I wanted to do was hold the trumpet to my lips and wail. Suddenly, the choir stopped and the conductor lowered his arms.

"Perfect," he said. "You should be proud of yourselves. Not a note out of place." And the look on everyone's face was beautiful. They were filled with their perfection.

I was so excited I just wanted to go somewhere and practice my trumpet. I wanted to be as perfect as they were and not have a note out of place. I went outside and began to spin around and around and when I stopped I was facing a tall building. It looked like the bell-tower part of an old cathedral. I ran over and it was full of people reading books. I knew I couldn't cut loose there so I took the elevator to the top and when I got out I snooped down the hall and found a small balcony, so I went out on it and looked across the city and saw all the places I had been walking.

The whole day I had been playing a big Pittsburgh board game called Are You Normal, Joey Pigza, or Are You Wired? I was just about to declare myself the winner when I realized there was one more place I hadn't pointed my finger. At me. The real test was inside me. I leaned back against the balcony wall, closed my eyes, and turned my head upside down. I took a deep breath and when I opened my eyes the whole city had flipped over and it reminded me that so far nothing on my trip had turned out as I had expected.

I had thought Dad would tell me all about his past. But he didn't want to talk about it, so I was wrong about that. I had thought there was some chance Mom and Dad might get back together, but Mom really didn't want to and Dad had a new girlfriend. So I was wrong about that. I had thought Grandma would be creepy, but she was only sad and sick now. So I was wrong about that too. And now I wasn't even wearing a patch, which was the scariest thing of all, but all day long I wasn't goofing up. I was totally in control of every second. Every thought. Every action. Every word. As Dad would say, "Today, I was on *top* of my game." I just smiled to myself, and thought all my troubles had vanished.

This is what it is like to be normal, I guessed. You don't have problems. Only messed-up people have problems, and since I wasn't messed up anymore I was free as a bird. I could just leap off the balcony, spread my arms, and soar through the Chicken Little sky which was not falling.

"I'm normal. I'm normal. I'm really normal. Joey Pigza is normal." I could stop thinking that bad things were always coming my way. I switched on my Herb Alpert tape. I slipped my speakers into my ears and pulled my trumpet out of my backpack. I stood up and started to play as loud as I could. And I kept playing until I looked at my watch and saw that it was time to meet Dad. I put my trumpet away and got going.

I had a huge smile on my face all the way down the elevator and across the street and all the way up the steps to the War Memorial building where Dad worked. Just when I reached the top Dad stepped out the door.

"Hey, buddy," he yelled out. "How was your big day?"

"It was perfect!" I shouted. "Awesome. The best day

I ever had. I felt like the most normal kid in the world. Now I just want more and more of these days. A year of them. A lifetime of them."

"See," he said. "I told you that patch was bogus."

"You were right," I said. "You made me better."

He got tears in his eyes and had to wipe them away with his long fingers.

"That's the greatest thing anyone ever said to me," he said. "Give me five."

I held out my hand and grinned at him.

"No way," he said, "I'm not falling for that again."

"I won't pull my hand back," I said. "Promise."

He tried to get the jump on me and took a big quick swing, but I still pulled my hand away in time and he lurched forward all over again. "You promised," he said.

I turned and jumped down the steps two at a time and laughed bent over until I thought I was going to cry too. When I looked up he was still standing at the top.

"I'll get you back," he said, in a voice that I wasn't sure was joking or serious. Either way, it made me feel nervous all over, which kind of put a tiny dent in my perfect day.

10

SECRET

"Mexico?" Mom repeated. "Ha! Who told you I was in Mexico?"

"Tiffany," I replied.

"I'm sure she was just trying to be helpful," Mom said. "But it's my guess that she couldn't find Mexico with a map." Then she lowered her voice. "I was doing something private. I was in traffic court. I didn't tell you but I got a ticket on my way back from Pittsburgh. Can you believe I was pulled over for driving erratically? I was dodging the holes and the cop thought I was drunk. Then he saw that my license was expired. So yesterday I had to go to court and pay a fine and now I have to wait thirty days for a new license."

"Oh," I said. "Sorry." I was the one had who told her to dodge the holes.

"Well, that's enough about me," she said. "What did

you do this last while? Have you made lots of new friends on the team?"

"No," I said. "I just pitch. I don't have to go to practice. They field and do all the hitting."

"Don't they let you hit?" she asked.

"They let me try," I replied. "I just haven't hit the ball yet. I swing, but so far I've whiffed every time."

"What about after the game?" Mom asked. "Do you go out and eat pizza?"

"No. Dad's the coach and so I just hang out with him and we eat pizza together."

"Well, I wish you'd make some friends," she said.

"I have Pablo," I replied.

"But you need to hang around kids your own age," she said.

"I'm different than they are," I said. "*You* always said so. You always said I was special."

"And you are," she said as if she had her arms around me. "But you can be my special Joey *and* have friends."

I knew what she was getting at. But it was hard making friends on a team when Dad was the coach. He yelled at everyone and when the games were over they took off. They didn't want to hang around and get yelled at anymore. But I knew Mom wanted to feel better so I said, "I'm working on it. There are a few nice kids I'm getting to know."

"Well, I'm glad to hear that, honey," she said. "You just be yourself and they'll like you even better."

Suddenly I remembered something good I wanted to say. "I pitched a whole game and won," I blurted out. "Now we're trying to win the championship. And yesterday I spent the whole day in Pittsburgh. It was the best day of my life. I love the city. There is so much to do and I had a blast."

"Was your dad with you?"

"No. He was working, but I was fine. I didn't go far and I didn't talk to strangers or do anything they tell you not to do on *Sesame Street*."

"Are you changing your medication?" she asked.

That was the question I didn't want her to ask and I got that spastic feeling all over my skin like when you slowly walk into an ice-cold swimming pool and your gooseflesh skin just wants to climb up your bones and hunch up on your shoulders.

"I played like I was a mannequin at a store," I said. "I put on some new clothes and sunglasses and stood next to a real mannequin till a lady noticed."

"Joey," she said, "are you changing your patch?"

"Then I went into a video arcade and had self-control."

"Joey, you aren't answering me. Have you changed your patch?"

"What do you think?" I said, and began to sputter

with laughter, and then I just kept finding different ways to laugh like a braying donkey and an insane hyena and a wacky chimpanzee and I laughed until I thought by the time I stopped laughing she would have forgotten what we were talking about. But she didn't go for it.

"Joey, don't play games with me," she said in a voice that was backing me into a corner.

"Yes," I said. "I changed it." And I had. I went from a patch to no patch. That was a change. But it was a lie too, and I wasn't laughing about that, because it was wrong.

"Let me talk with your dad," she said sternly.

I held the receiver by the cord and swung it around like a soap-on-a-rope. "Dad," I hollered across the room. "Mom wants you."

He came over quickly and snatched the phone out of the air. He put his hand over the mouthpiece and whispered to me, "You didn't tell her about our little secret?"

"No," I mouthed.

"Good boy," he said, and winked at me. "Hi, Fran," he said smoothly. "How was Mexico?"

I don't think she talked much about Mexico. Because all Dad said was, "Don't worry. Everything is under control. He's having the time of his life. It's good for him to live in a man's world. He'll make friends, but for now he and I are spending lots of time together. And don't worry about the medication. I've got it under control."

When he gave the phone back to me he opened the refrigerator and pulled out a beer.

"I'm going to work," he said. "When I get home, be ready for the game tonight."

I gave him the thumbs-up even though it worried me to see him having a beer for breakfast, and when I put the phone to my ear it sounded like Mom was grinding her teeth. "I have a little secret," I whispered.

"What?" she asked in her I've-had-it-with-you voice, like she just wanted me to spit it out. "What?"

"It's a secret," I said. "But when I tell you what it is you'll be stunned."

"Well, stun me now," she said. "Hit me with your best shot."

"Not now," I sang. "As they say, the best things in life are worth waiting for."

"Don't play games with me, young man," she insisted.

"Okay," I said. "I'm going now. Goodbye." I put down the phone and went to my room thinking that when I tell her the secret she'll really be surprised and then she won't yell at me anymore.

On my way through the living room Grandma stopped me.

"Do you have any of that telephone money left that your mom gave you?" she asked.

"Yes," I said. "A little."

"Well, run down to the store and part with some of it and get me a pack of generics."

"But they're killing you," I pleaded.

"Nonsense. You just don't want to part with any of that phone money. You're too cheap to spend a couple bucks on your old grandma."

"Okay," I said.

"And I'll call and tell them you're coming," she said. "I just don't want to ride that buggy down and all the way back. I'm too winded."

I dug the money out of my pillowcase, grabbed my trumpet, and ordered Pablo to follow me.

"Hurry back," Grandma hollered from the couch.

"March behind me," I ordered Pablo as we left the house. "A one, a two, a one, two, three, four!" I put the trumpet to my lips and tried to blast out the long first note from "El Garbanzo" and off we went, down the sidewalk. I took huge giant steps like I was leading a parade and wearing a fancy outfit with gold buttons and one of those white hats with a tall fluffy gold feather sticking out the top. I tried to play and march without the metal mouthpiece cracking my front teeth in half and Pablo had to take twenty baby steps to my one in order to keep up.

At the store the lady clerk had already set the cigarettes on the counter. I gave her the money and she put them in a bag. We turned right around and started home.

Now I was trying to play "Love Potion No. 9" until I started singing, "I held my nose, I closed my eyes . . . I took a drink!" Then I ran around kissing "everything in sight" just like the guy in the old song. I kissed a mailbox, a telephone pole, a stop sign, and a tree trunk. Pablo didn't kiss anything but he did do his business in someone's front yard and then got snappish with a toy poodle and I had to separate them and a lady came out of the house and yelled at me for what Pablo did in her yard and I yelled "Sorry" and grabbed Pablo with one arm and ran down the street and after I had turned left and right a few times I didn't know where I was.

I put Pablo down on the road. "Okay, troublemaker," I said. "Sniff out how to get home." He sniffed a pebble and looked up at me with his squinty lizard face and I could tell he had no idea either.

We walked around in the sun for a while, which made my head hot. I was nervous that the dogcatcher might come looking for us because Pablo was off his leash. Then I saw a police car and ducked because I didn't want to get arrested for having cigarettes. Finally I saw the oxygen tank delivery truck and knew it had to be going to our house. I picked Pablo up again and tucked him under one arm like a football and my trumpet under the other and ran until I came to a corner that I recognized and then I knew how to get home from there.

"Where've you been?" Grandma asked when I opened the front door. "I'm here having a nicotine fit, darn near climbing the walls, and you run off to the end of the earth."

"I got lost," I said. "I took a wrong turn."

"I've heard that excuse before. Whenever you used to get lost coming home from school, I knew to expect you were slipping into a bad spell. And sure enough, you couldn't keep your mind on what you were doing and ran around like the devil was poking you with his pitchfork all night long."

"I'm not that way anymore," I said. "I'm different. I've changed. I'm better. I spent the whole day in Pittsburgh and was fine."

"That tells me nothing," she said. "People in Pittsburgh are nuts, so how could you tell if you weren't too?"

I looked over at Pablo. He was lapping pop out of her glass she had set on the rug and that made me smile.

She unwrapped the pack and began to tap a cigarette out the top. "You might fool yourself, but you can't fool Grandma," she said, and struck a match.

"You're just trying to scare me like before," I shot back.

"No," she wheezed, putting her cigarette down and reaching for her oxygen. "I'm trying to scare some sense into you *now*."

I didn't want to listen to her anymore and she knew it. I put the trumpet to my lips and let out a crazy duck sound.

"Okay," she said. "I've said my piece. Now, get some forks. I heated up a snack for us, but it's probably cold by now."

I set out the TV tables like I used to do when we lived together and then she tuned the TV to *The Price Is Right* and a lady was making a decision between choosing a car, picking what was behind door number three, or taking the big wad of cash.

I got a little jumpy when screaming "Take the cash! Take the cash!" and when the lady picked door number three and only got a roomful of ice cream sandwiches I threw up my arms and knocked over my TV table. It fell forward and my chicken potpie hit the carpet and exploded like someone had upchucked a bucket of yellow slime and peas and carrots and burnt crust.

"Klutz!" Grandma snapped as Pablo started to lap it up.

"Don't eat that, Pablo," I said. "That's like eating throw-up."

"It's not throw-up," she snapped back. "Only throw-up can be throw-up." Grandma stood and poked her foot under Pablo's tummy and flicked him into the air. "Bad dog!" she shouted as he flipped around. I lunged forward to catch him but missed and belly flopped onto the potpie mess and slid forward like I had hit an oil slick. Pablo landed on my back and I started to laugh so hard because it was like we were a circus clown act and as I laughed Pablo barked and ran circles around the rug and Grandma pursed her lips and nodded like she had seen it all before.

"Mark my words," she said. "You're slippin' back to your old self."

"I only fell," I said. "I'll clean it up so Dad won't get mad."

"It's not the cleaning up that concerns me," she said. "It's you getting that wired look again with your eyes spinning around all over the place."

I got up and went to the bathroom to wash. But really, what Grandma had said bothered me because I wanted to be the new me and not the old me. I stood in front of the mirror and stared into my eyes. She was wrong. They didn't spin. But the room did so I pulled the T-shirt up over my head. "I'm fine," I said to myself. And I was.

That night my first pitch went right down the middle of the plate about waist high and the kid swung the bat only after it had already smacked into the catcher's glove. A perfect pitch. I looked over at Dad.

He was shaking his head and I thought I could hear the gears turning as he was trying to figure out how to get Mom to let me live with him. All the way over in the car that's all he could talk about. He called me and Leezy his "second-chance family" and went on and on about how he wouldn't make the same mistakes he did with Mom. I asked if he had told Mom and Leezy about all this and he said he was working out the details and figured he needed to visit Humpty Dumpty to do some thinking.

My next pitch was a called strike, and the third one was about nose high, but by then the guy was so desperate he would have swung at one ten feet over his head. The next guy popped out. And the next one grounded to first.

I was sitting in the dugout with my hat pulled down over my face when Leezy came over. "Hey, caveman," she said, lifting my hat. "You look sharp out there tonight."

"Thanks," I replied.

Then she leaned over and gave me a hug. "Your dad told me the good news that you want all of us to live together," she said, looking at me like she was practicing a happy face for clown school.

"What does that mean?" I asked.

"That maybe your dad and me would live together and you would too."

"That wasn't *my* idea," I blurted out. "It was *his*."

And I pointed to Dad, who was pacing a dirt path in the grass down the third-base line.

"Well, no matter who thought of it first, I think it's a fantastic idea."

"I already have a mom," I said, and took a deep breath and didn't stop until I was dying to breathe out as if I could blow her away like the wolf did to the pig's straw house.

"I wouldn't replace your mom," she said. "Nobody could do that. I just mean that I'd love it if you lived with us. And I sure know your dad is excited about it."

"He's excited about *everything*," I said.

"That's what I like about him," she said. "He's a nut."

"What about Grandma?" I asked, and looked over into the stands where she was sitting with her oxygen tank on one side and Pablo on the other.

"Your dad thinks she needs assisted living," Leezy said. "You know, a place where she can get constant medical attention."

I wasn't sure what that meant, but it couldn't be good. "And Pablo?"

"Oh, he can stay," she said cheerfully. "Everyone loves Pablo."

That part of what she said was true. But it wasn't true that I already loved the whole idea of living with her and Dad. And I knew Mom wouldn't love it either.

"Do you want a pizza?" she asked, and held up the phone. "Would that make you feel a little better?"

Everything that would make me feel better would make everyone else feel worse. Ever since I had lied to Mom, I hadn't felt good about myself. "Can I use your phone?" I asked her. "I want to call home."

"Sure," she said, and handed it to me.

I pressed the little numbers and held it to my ear. Mom answered.

"Hi," I said. "I'm pitching."

"Where are you?" she asked.

"In the dugout."

"Honey, that's wonderful," she said, and began to laugh.

"Why are you laughing?" I asked.

"Because I think it is great that you and your dad are getting along and that you are on a team and doing so well. I'm just so proud of you."

"Thanks," I said.

"I'm glad you called but you better keep your mind on the game."

"I have something to tell you," I said.

"What?"

I wanted to tell her my secret, and I wanted to tell her that Dad was drinking beer for breakfast and planning for me to live with him and Leezy, but I didn't want to ruin her mood. So I said, "I love you."

"I love you too," she said.

Just then Leezy waved her hand in my face. "Time to pitch," she whispered.

I hopped up. "Gotta pitch," I said. "Bye." I pushed past Leezy and ran toward the mound.

It didn't take me long to get the first guy out. But after two strikes to the second batter I lowered my hands. "Can I call a time-out?" I asked the ump.

"Time-out!" he hollered.

Dad looked horrified, like I had just fallen in front of a moving truck. He ran out to the mound. "Are you hurt?" he asked.

"Why did you tell Leezy that all of us living together was *my* idea?"

"I was just trying to soften her up," he said. "You know, make her feel like you wanted her to live with us too."

"Well, I didn't say it, you did. So you should tell her she's wrong."

"I will," he said. "Right after the game. I promise. Now, no more time-outs," he said.

"And no more saying I said things I didn't," I said.

"Okay. Chill out. Now just pitch. We'll talk about it later."

"We never talk," I said. "I only listen."

"Well, you're talking plenty now," he said.

"You're on my mound," I said. "I'm the boss here."

“Okay, boss. Pitch,” he replied, then walked off talking to himself.

“And one more thing,” I said.

“What?” he hollered, spinning around.

“No more beer for breakfast or I’ll tell Mom.”

“Hey, it doesn’t hurt me, and what she doesn’t know won’t hurt her,” he said harshly. “Now don’t ruin the game for me. Just pitch.” Then he walked back to the third-base coach’s box.

When I turned around, the rest of the team was staring at me like I was the weird one. I didn’t want to ruin things for them either. So I just pitched. I got that batter out. And the rest of them too. And even though we won the game I didn’t feel like a winner for some reason.

11

JELLY LEGS

"You need to get some fresh air," Grandma said, exhaling a cloud of smoke. "You've been moping around and fidgeting and driving me and Pablo nuts. Why don't you go outside and wind your spring down."

"Do you want to play golf?" I asked her.

"No. Last time I almost yanked my nose off. Since then I've decided I'm of the age where I just smoke cigarettes and watch TV."

"Can I push you around in your buggy?"

"Why don't you go pester Carter?" she said. "Maybe you two can go to town again."

"Forget town," Carter called out from the hallway. "I been thinking about something better—a place I been wanting to go."

"What about work?" I asked.

"To heck with work," he said as he entered the living room. "How long can you change lightbulbs and mop floors before you go bonkers? That job would drive a normal man insane."

"Then you must be *abnormal*," Grandma cracked. "It only drives you to drink."

Dad flashed her an angry look. "How about we all go bungee jumping?"

"If I dove off a bridge it'd take the last of my breath away," Grandma said, sucking on her mouthpiece.

"Just what I had in mind," Dad mumbled with his voice trailing off toward the door.

I hopped up onto the couch, and kept hopping until I hopped on the cushion where Pablo had burrowed and he growled. "I've always wanted to go bungee jumping," I said.

"Come on," Dad said. "Let's crank it up."

On the way over in the car he said, "Now don't tell your mom we did this. Bungee jumping is one of those guy things she might not understand."

"Okay," I replied, and thought, I won't be able to tell Mom anything that I did with Dad. She'll pick me up and ask, "How'd it go?" and I'll say, "Fine," and she'll say, "What all'd you do?" and I'll say, "Stuff," and she'll ask, "Did you do anything special?" and I'll say, "No," and she'll keep asking until finally she'll give up talking to a wall.

We drove outside the city and passed through farm country. I had my face pressed to the glass so I could see everything. There were cows and tractors and barns and people working. Rows of corn and beans and fields of melons were planted. Dad pointed out everything. He knew it all because his dad had been a farmer. "I should have been a farmer too," he said. "But plants just grew too slow for me and when I was old enough I went into the city to chase after the fast life."

I had a hard time imagining Dad, or Grandma, living on a farm. "What happened then?" I asked.

"I burned out," he said. "All my energy went into bad habits and drinking and running around and it seems I was always on the go, but I didn't get anything done but mess up my life."

"Where did you meet Mom?" I asked.

"In a restaurant," he replied. "I was learning how to be a bartender and she was a waitress and it just went from there."

Finally we pulled up to an old railroad bridge that spanned a wide gorge. Dad parked and we got out. In the middle of the bridge was a tall crane and a group of people all leaning over the rail. As Dad and I walked toward them I looked over the edge of the bridge. Down below was a creek filled with round, dark boulders. One of them had a skull and crossbones painted on the top. The crane operator lowered a kid whose jump was over and as he reached the ground a man in an orange vest and hard hat grabbed him and began to unstrap him from the harness. Then the crane brought the harness back up.

"See the skull?" Dad said, pointing. "Do you suppose that's where some loser flattened his head?"

"Are you trying to scare me?" I asked.

"Yes," he said, and smiled. "I'm trying to pull you out from thinking that you need your medicine again. You got to let that idea go. You are fine. Sometimes, when you stop taking medicine, it just takes a while to adjust and you get worse before you get better."

"Is that why you're smoking more now?" I asked.

He peered down at me. "Yeah," he said. "Any day I expect I'll wake up and kick the habit."

"Is that true?" I asked.

"Sure it is," he said. "If I didn't think so I'd jump off this bridge without the cord."

There were a few people in line and we joined them and watched. Everyone was a little nervous, which helped me feel more comfortable. A teenager was being placed in the harness and then the bungee cord was snapped to a metal ring on his back. He climbed a set of wooden steps and stood on the railing of the bridge.

"Count to three and dive for the skull," the instructor said.

The kid counted and screamed from the moment he dove until he stopped bouncing.

"I don't think they have this ride at Disney World,"

Dad said, grinning, and his usual little smile was wide open.

Each time someone jumped I felt the bottom drop out of my belly like a trapdoor. I watched them all bounce up and down with their arms and legs in a panic, and when they stopped and were unhooked they fell over to the side and only after a few minutes did they manage to stand like newborn horses and stagger up the hill.

"Jelly legs," Dad said. "You get it from being scared. Once, I joined the army to get away from the booze and in basic training they used to fire live rounds over our heads, and that spooked me so bad I couldn't even use my legs to crawl. This should be good."

I thought so too. My legs were already shaking and I hadn't done anything but watch.

"How long were you in the army?" I asked.

"About eight weeks," he said, and shrugged. "That too was not a marriage made in heaven."

Someone let out an awful scream and we all lunged for the rail and looked over the side expecting the worst. But it was nothing unusual. Just another bouncing person begging to get down. When we looked back it was our turn.

"You go first," I said to Dad.

"Monkey see, monkey do," he replied, and stepped forward. He bought two tickets and we both had to sign a piece of paper that said it wasn't their fault if we died. They fitted Dad with the harness and snapped the hook onto the ring. He climbed up the steps and stood on the rail. "Humpty Dumpty sat on a wall," he recited. "Humpty Dumpty had a great fall. All the king's horses and all the king's men couldn't put that ol' egg back together again." When he finished he reached into his back pocket and slipped out a small brown bottle. He unscrewed the cap and drank it all down. Then he tossed the bottle to the man. "Can you put this in the trash?"

"You need a bigger bottle," the man said, and tossed it into a bucket. "Especially if you're trying to work up some courage."

"Just a little medicine," Dad replied, and winked at me as he wiped his lips with the back of his hand. Then he dove backward. I looked over the edge and watched him plunge to the bottom with his arms crossed over his chest like he was already dead, but when he bounced up he wiggled his arms and legs and began to sing, "The itsy-bitsy spider went up the waterspout, down came the rain and washed the spider out." And that's what he sang, bouncing up and down, until finally he came to a stop. The crane lowered him toward the ground and the man below hauled him in and unhooked him.

Dad took one step, then plopped down on his rear

end. He cupped his hands around his mouth. "Jelly legs!" he yelled.

By then I was strapped into the harness and the long bungee cord was hauled up by the crane and snapped onto my ring. "What happens if this breaks?" I asked.

"We all run for the hills," the man said with a straight face. Then he laughed. "I don't know. It's never happened before."

"There's always a first time," I said right back.

"That can be arranged," he replied, "but it will cost you extra."

I climbed up the steps and stood on the rail. I looked straight out at the curved horizon and felt like a pirate walking the plank. I wished Pablo was with me.

"Dive forward on the count of three," he ordered. "One, two—"

"Two and a half," I cut in. I was totally hyper and I couldn't tell if I needed a patch or if I needed to come to my senses. You didn't need to be wired to feel hyper.

"Three," the man said, and clapped his hands. "Jump!"

I closed my eyes and because my legs had already turned to jelly I couldn't spring forward, so I just stepped off. I screamed all the way down and I screamed with each bounce. And I was still a nervous wreck when the man below unclipped me and handed me to Dad.

"You okay, buddy?" he asked. "You look like Casper the Ghost." He had to hold me upright by the back of my shirt because my legs were liquid.

"Let's do it again," I said, panting. "This is just what I need."

"You sure?" Dad asked.

"Totally," I said, with my voice quivering. "This is the best I've felt all day."

"Okay, but don't mess up your arm for tonight," he warned me. "Or I'll throw you off without the cord. And then Leezy will throw me off."

So we each jumped five more times and all the fear and falling and screaming wiped out every hyper feeling I had and when we got home I was exhausted and went directly to my room and threw myself onto my bed and it was as if I had fallen one more time, only straight down an endless black hole.

The next thing I knew Dad was waking me. "Jump up," he said, and tugged on my ear. "Time to get ready for the game. The *big* game." He whistled. "The semi-finals. How's your arm?"

"Fine," I said, rubbing the sleep from my eyes.

"Legs?"

I stood up and squatted down then sprang forward like a frog. "Good," I said. "The jelly's all gone."

"Great," he said, rubbing his hands together. "Well, get dressed and let's go kick some butt."

"Yeah," I said, and felt all foggy inside. "Yeah. Who are we playing?"

"This is the semifinals, bud," he said. "Snap to it. We're playing a team that kicked us around before you got here. And now we're going to return the favor. Now let's get a move on."

He left and I opened my closet and pulled my uniform off the hanger. I hadn't let Grandma wash it yet, but it didn't smell too bad. I unballed the dirty white sweat socks out of my high-top baseball cleats and put them on. I double knotted the laces, then stood up.

I looked into the mirror and flicked my hair over my little bald spot. But it wouldn't cover it right. So I flicked it over again, then again and again. And before long that pink spot started to itch so I began to scratch it until I could begin to feel the skin heat up and get shiny like something being polished. And it kept itching even more, so I turned my finger just a bit and caught the edge of my nail on the skin and that felt good until I couldn't stop and finally the skin split open but it wasn't so much blood that leaked out as it was fluid like what comes out of a blister. Even then I couldn't stop and I rubbed it a little more until the spot burned like when you put a match out with your fingertips and I stood up on my tiptoes and rubbed harder until the itch was on fire and I could think of nothing else, and feel nothing else and imagine nothing else but that burning spot which was just getting hotter and hotter until I finally yanked my hand away and jammed it into my pocket and stood there twisting my hips around like pipe cleaners and hating myself just like old times and suddenly I knew for certain the other Joey had started to catch up to me and I wondered what to do about it. I spun around as if my old self was walking through the door. But he wasn't. He was already inside me. I reached for my book and took the used patch I had saved and rubbed it up and down on the inside of my arm. I kept rubbing until the skin underneath hurt, and I kept hoping that there was a little medicine left in it. But it didn't feel that way and suddenly Dad yelled out, "Hey, bud, you ready or what?"

"One sec," I yelled back. I opened my dresser drawer and pulled a couple Band-Aids out of my bag of bathroom supplies. I unbuttoned my shirt and taped the patch to my belly. Here we go again, I said to myself. I knew it was going to be bad. How bad, I didn't know just yet. But I never forgot how I had been, so I didn't have to guess too much at what I'd become. My only hope was that Dad was right and I was just getting a little worse before I turned the corner and got better.

"What are you doing in there?" Dad asked. "Come on, we got a date with destiny."

My hands were shaking as I buttoned my shirt. I screwed my baseball cap on and opened the door. "I'm ready," I announced, and smiled my big smile, the one that always makes people think I'm okay when inside I'm ready to pop.

"That's my caveman," Dad said. He put down his beer bottle and curled his arm around my shoulder as we marched for the car.

"I've been thinking," he said, as soon as the car door closed. "Once you win this game I want to get my skull tattoo reworked, and if you want you can get your ear pierced."

"I want to," I said, fiddling with my earlobe, "but Mom doesn't want me to."

"What are you? A mama's boy? Get it pierced."

"I shouldn't," I said. "I told Mom I wouldn't."

"Look, your dog's ear is pierced, so why not yours?"

"That was an accident—"

"Some accidents are good," he said. "Like you."

"What do you mean?" I asked. But instantly I knew what he meant because I knew what it meant when parents called their kids "accidents." It meant they didn't plan for them, and probably didn't want them, that they were mistakes. And when Dad said "accident" it made me think I was less than wanted when I arrived—and suddenly I remembered when we were at Storybook Land he laughed at the Old Lady Who Lived in a Shoe and said she had a "few too many accidents."

"Joey," Dad said, "just chill. I didn't mean anything by it."

"I want to call Mom," I said. "I want to ask her if I was an accident."

"She'll tell you the same thing I have," he insisted. "You were a happy accident."

"If it was so happy how come you took off?"

"Because I wasn't happy," he said. "I was messed up."

"And what are you now?" I asked.

"Better," he said. "I think you're rubbing off on me in a good way."

He reached out to rub my head but I scooted across the seat to my door. I didn't talk to him anymore and instead flicked the automatic door lock up and down about a million times because it was better to listen to that click, click, clicking sound than to him saying over and over that I wasn't an accident.

As soon as the car stopped in the parking lot I grabbed my gym bag and jumped out. "Come back," he called. "It was an accident that I called you an accident." But by then I was headed for the bathroom where there was a pay phone.

"Think about this, Joey," he hollered behind me. "Would I want you here now if it wasn't my plan to keep you for good?"

That's all I heard because after that I was only listening to my cleats crunching the gravel and the sound of my breath sucking in and pushing out. I wanted to call Mom and ask her if I was an accident but I didn't have any phone money on me so I turned around. I lowered my head and kept walking. I passed Dad. I passed the players. I walked all the way out to the mound and marched around and around the edge and stomped the dirt down flat and nobody bothered me until the catcher threw me the ball and I threw a few warm-up pitches then said, "I'm ready."

The other team batted first.

"Come on, caveman," Dad hollered. "Bury this kid."

I lobbed an easy one in there and the batter knocked it out of the park.

"Time-out," Dad yelled to the umpire, and trotted out to the mound. "Something wrong?" he asked.

"It was an *accident*," I said, and smiled. "A mistake."

"Joey, we can talk about that later," he said. "But for now, just pitch the ball." He turned and trotted to the coach's box.

I walked the next batter. And the next one.

"Time-out," Dad called. He trotted out to the mound again. "What's the problem?"

"Get me Leezy's telephone," I said. "I want to call Mom."

"Not now, Joey," Dad said impatiently.

"Either I call Mom now, or I'll walk the whole team," I replied.

"What's gotten into you?" he asked angrily. "Huh?"

"You," I said.

He sighed. Then he held up a finger to the ump. "Family emergency!" he yelled as he ran over to Leezy, pulled the phone out of her purse, and returned.

"Stand outside my circle," I said to him as I took the phone, then dialed the number. He backed away.

"Hi, Mom," I said when she picked up, and before she could say anything I blurted out, "Was I an accident?"

"What are you talking about?" she asked.

"You know, was I a baby accident you didn't want?"

"No," she said right back. "No. Not at all. Who told you that?"

I could tell she was getting mad. Really mad. "Dad told me," I said. "Do you want to speak to him?"

"Yes," she said harshly. "Put him on."

I held out the phone like it was a stick of dynamite with a lit fuse. Dad reached for it. He turned away from me and they had a few sharp words and finally he growled, "We don't have all night to discuss this. We're standing on the mound in the middle of a play-off game." In a moment he handed me the phone.

"Joey," Mom said, changing the subject, "are you taking your medication?"

"Yeah," I replied. "I have a patch on right now."

"Then listen to your father, Joey. I'm sure he can't be happy with you talking on the phone during a game. And I'm not either. Now give your father back the phone and play ball. We'll talk later. Okay? Call me after the game."

"Okay," I said. "I just want to know that I'm more than an accident."

"You're my reason for living, breathing, and grinding my teeth," she said with a laugh. "Now mow those players down and bring that trophy home for me."

"Okay," I said. I handed Dad the phone. "I feel better."

"No more tricks," he warned me. "Or else."

He walked off as the umpire was walking toward the mound and the other coach was yelling and the players were shouting at us from the dugout and even some parents were booing and calling for us to forfeit the game.

But after Dad left I settled down and struck out the side and that made everyone quiet. I went back to the dugout and sat with my hat down over my face. Then I remembered I had my tape player in my bag so I got it out and ran the wires up the back of my shirt and put the speakers in my ears and turned it on really loud. I started rocking back and forth and scratching at my head again.

"Hey," Leezy said, surprising me as she tugged a speaker out of my ear. "What's wrong with your noggin? You're scratching like you got a family of fleas up there."

"Yeah," I said, and lifted the hat off my face. "I have fleas. Pablo gave them to me."

"Well, we'll get a flea collar for you," she said. "And a matching one for Pablo too."

I smiled.

"Your dad said you're nervous," she ventured. "Anything I can do to help?"

According to Dad I was supposed to help myself. I knew she was trying to be nice to me and I wanted to be nice back, but there wasn't anything in me that wanted to talk. My mouth was dry and I just felt itchy all over and the only thing that made me feel better was the music. So I covered my face with my hat, jammed the little speakers even deeper inside my ears, and nodded along, and that was good until she tapped me on the shoulder and pointed to the mound.

"You're on," she mouthed.

I stood up and lifted my hat. I shoved the tape player into my back pocket and ran out to the mound and with the Brass playing "Tangerine" it seemed that I wasn't nervous at all and I calmed down and just pitched and kept getting batters out and rolling along. Our team scored a few runs and I kept their team from doing any damage. But by the fifth inning my tape player batteries started to wear down and the songs got all loopy and I started to feel loopy too. I had two strikes on a batter when I looked over to Dad.

"Time-out!" I hollered, and popped the speakers out of my ears.

Dad trotted up to the mound. "What is it this time?" he asked.

"I need new batteries," I said.

"For your arm?" he asked.

"My tape player." I turned around and showed him the player in my back pocket and the wires running up my shirt and out my neck. "It helps me concentrate," I said.

"You just don't want to hear me hollering at you," he replied.

"I don't like it when you yell," I said, agreeing. "I'm just trying to do my best."

"Then just *pitch*," he said. "And I won't yell. This isn't a dance. It's a baseball game."

"No batteries," I said, "no pitching." I held out the ball for him.

"Come on," the ump called out. "Let's keep the game moving."

"Give me an inning to get them, Joey," Dad said. "Be reasonable. I don't have batteries in my pocket."

"Okay," I replied. "One inning." Dad ran back to the coach's box and I struck the batter out.

By the time I returned to the bench and scratched my itchy spot some more, Leezy ran up with four batteries.

"Joey," she asked, and pointed to my head, "are you telling me the truth about you being okay?"

I loaded the batteries in my tape player. "Giant fleas," I said.

"Your head's bleeding," she replied, and tried to touch me, but I hopped up and put my hat on.

After I struck out and our team scored a few more runs I went back out to the mound. We had a four-run lead when I looked over to Dad and smiled. He smiled back and looked very happy. I waved to him. He waved back.

"Time-out!" I yelled, and turned my tape player off.

Dad ran straight at me like a bull.

"What is it this time?" he asked.

"I want to have a conversation," I said. "It's been bothering me that I came all this way to see you but you never told me why you never came to see me."

"You want to talk about this now?" he snarled, spitting out his words and jabbing at me with his finger. "You spend the entire day with me and you don't say boo and now you want to talk?"

"That's because you do all the talking," I said.

"Well, I'm not talking now," he replied. "No way. Pitch!"

"Come on, son," the ump hollered. "This is your final warning. We can't do this all night. Either you play or you pack it up."

"Bring me Pablo," I said. "I want Pablo with me."

"Let's go," the ump said.

"Pablo," I repeated. "Get him."

"Next inning," Dad said with his face as tight as a fist. "And you can throw him for strikes for all I care."

The ump started toward the mound. "One more time-out," he threatened, "and the kid is ejected."

"Don't blow this for me," Dad said under his breath. "Or else."

I turned the music back on as he pranced away with his arms and legs slapping together like a set of wind chimes. Once he was back in the coach's box and the umpire took his place, I went into my windup then rolled the ball all the way to the plate.

"Strike!" I yelled, and threw my arms up into the air like a champion.

"This isn't bowling!" Dad hollered.

"I'm throwing strikes," I yelled back, and I knew I had got him just about as mad as I wanted him to be, so then I pitched real strikes the rest of the inning. And a few innings later, when I finished the game, I had my tape player blaring and Pablo inside my shirt curled up like a beer belly hanging over my belt. We won six to three but Dad looked like he had fallen off the bungee bridge without the cord and I felt the same way.

The first thing he said to me when I came to the dugout was, "You are going to drive me to drink."

"Don't be mad at me," I said. "I need some medicine."

"You're taking this *hyper* thing too far," he said angrily. "You don't need medicine. You need to get a grip on yourself."

"Fine," I said. "I'll get a grip." I wrapped my arms around myself and spun around in circles. Dad grabbed me by the shoulders and I squirmed away and did a jagged little dance while he tried to settle me down.

"Okay, boys," Leezy ordered, and got her arms between us. "Let's walk it off." She turned him around and shoved him toward the scoreboard.

"Dad," I yelled, and stuck out my hand. "Give me five and let's make up."

"Don't push your luck, Joey," he said, looking back over his shoulder. "I've had enough of your tricks for one night."

Leezy reached out and took my hand. "Time to go home," she said calmly. "You've had a long day."

It had been long. And Grandma and Pablo and me got into Leezy's car and she dropped us off. I don't know where Dad went. I forgot about calling Mom and ran to my room and untied one shoe but I got a knot in my other shoe and I tried picking at it but I had chewed my fingernails down so low I couldn't pick the laces apart and after a while I couldn't even try and my hands were shaking so hard I lost patience. I started pulling on the laces and I knew the knot was getting smaller and tighter but I couldn't stop myself from just wanting to rip it open. Finally I just let out a yowl, then took my shirt off and whipped it across the room. I went to bed with my one shoe and pants on and even though I was sleepy I couldn't sleep. I kept thinking of the movie *Invasion of the Body Snatchers* and figured I shouldn't ever fall asleep again. Because instead of waking up like a zombie as they did in the movie, I'd wake up *wired*.

12

SCARY-BOOK LAND

The next morning I woke up feeling like half me and half not, like when you mix baking soda and vinegar together and come up with a totally weird third thing. Well, that's what I felt like, something not yet named. A fizzy experiment.

Plus my shoe was still on my foot.

"Come on, Cinderella, the ball game is over," Grandma announced six inches from my ear. She was standing over me and dangling Pablo by his hind paws so he could lick my face.

"Where's Dad?" I asked, and licked Pablo right back.

"Still celebrating," Grandma said. "He didn't come home, and I need to get to the doctors'."

"For what?" I asked.

"Measure my lungs," she rasped. "They make me

breathe into a machine and can tell if I'm breathing better."

"But you're still smoking," I said. "Aren't you getting worse?"

"No. Sometimes you can get better," she said. "I had a friend who claimed smoking two packs a day kept her from getting cancer."

"Sounds like a nut case," I remarked.

She pointed toward my feet and raised an eyebrow. "Look who's talking," she said, and began to sing. "Diddle, diddle, dumpling, my son John. Went to bed with his trousers on. One shoe off, and one shoe on—"

She couldn't finish because she began to cough.

"Do you want me to help you get to the doctors'?" I asked as I stood up.

"Yes," she croaked. "That would be nice."

"Then I can be Mr. Nice," I said.

I hobbled into the kitchen and got a steak knife, then squatted down and cut through the knot in my laces. I pulled my shoe and uniform pants off, then went into the bedroom and put on my jeans and a T-shirt and sneakers.

Grandma was waiting for me on the porch. "The bus stop is a long ways off," she said, and handed me a blueberry Pop-Tart plastered in white icing. "But the bus goes right by the clinic."

I set up the step stool and got her into the buggy.

Once she was situated on her couch cushion I fixed her oxygen tank against her side. I put Pablo in his baby seat and settled him down with the Pop-Tart, slipped the stool under the buggy, and we were off.

The bus stop was a concrete bench long past the convenience store. The only shade was from the metal pole with the bus-stop sign. It was hot and Pablo's face was covered with melted Pop-Tart icing. I got Grandma out and sat her on the bench. She put on her giant sunglasses and said, "Hide the buggy and stool in the bushes so we have it when we get back." She pointed toward an empty field of weeds and shrubs. I did what she told me to do because it was better than anything I told myself to do.

When I sat next to her I said, "I need some medicine."

"So do I," she said. "Maybe the doctor can fix us both up."

"Yeah," I said.

"You nervous?" she asked and reached across to brush some hair over the scab on my head.

"I'm always nervous," I replied.

"I mean about the game," she said. "You nervous about losing?"

"I suppose. But I'm more worried about what to do if I lose it out there and if Dad starts getting mental and calling me names and I just react and go nuts."

"I guess you'll soon find out," she said.

"Yep," I replied, and sighed as if my lungs too had sprung a leak. "I will."

"I guess because I'm sick now I think back on a lot of good times we had together," she said. Her lips were all dried from breathing through her mouth and her twisted smile looked like something pried open with a screwdriver. "Remember the time I broke the broom handle in half and taped a piece to each of your legs because I thought it would slow you down?"

"Yeah," I said. It wasn't funny before but now it seemed funny.

"But it didn't slow you down. You just stomped stiff-legged around like a hyper Frankenstein."

I laughed because somehow I'd ended up outside and the neighbor lady thought Grandma had finally broken both my legs. She wanted to rush me to the doctor and kept saying, "Come here and tell me what happened." So finally I went right up to her ear and yelled, "I'm a monster!" then clomped off, and she didn't follow me.

"And remember the time you climbed in the washer and turned it on. If you weren't screaming so loud I wouldn'ta found you until that rotor had beaten you into butter."

I laughed again. But it was the kind of "ha, ha, ha" laugh that sounds more like a grownup being polite after someone tells an unfunny joke. I wished I could give out a real bellyaching laugh but that washing machine had hurt and before I knew it my fake laugh turned into saying "Ouch, ouch, ouch," like I was being battered back and forth all over again.

I was relieved when the bus arrived and we slowly got on. Grandma rode for free because she was a senior, and I rode for free because she told the driver I was under six. We were the only passengers. I put Grandma in a seat for the disabled and put Pablo next to her. He wasn't disabled but he wasn't normal either.

I stood so I could hold onto a pole and spin around. After a while I figured out a game to keep me busy. I pushed the STOP bar and ran up to the front door.

"Stay behind the yellow line," the driver said to me because I hadn't.

"Okay," I replied.

As soon as he came to a stop and opened the front doors I ran down the steps and dashed along the bus to the back doors which I pulled open and hopped right back on again and took a seat and bobbed my head back and forth and wiggled my butt and whistled. Granny just gave me a head-shaking you'd-better-watch-your-step look, but I gave her an innocent look in return and soon stood up in the aisle and bus-surfed as I stumbled and swooped forward like I was riding a huge wave in Hawaii. Then when I spotted the next bus-stop bench I pressed the STOP bar and I could see the driver peering back at me in his big mirror.

"Time to stop!" I hollered. "Got places to go and people to meet!"

The bus driver glared at me and I looked over at Grandma and Pablo. "Ask," she hissed, "if there is a smoking section on this bus."

"Hey, driver!" I yelled forward. "Is there a smoking section on the bus?"

The driver turned around. "Yeah. We got two. One on the front bumper and one on the rear bumper. Take your pick." Then he laughed to himself.

"Funny," Grandma rumbled, and began to tap out a cigarette from her pack.

"Are you going to smoke?" I asked.

"Yeah," she said. "What's he gonna do? Throw an old invalid off the bus? Just let him try and I'll have Pablo nibble him to death."

The driver didn't pull over at the next stop, so I stood up and pressed the STOP bar again and again until the buzzer was almost a nonstop sound.

"I need to get off for real!" I hollered.

Finally the driver swung the bus over to a stop. I hopped down the stairs and turned to run to the back door. But the doors wouldn't pull open and in a panic I ran back toward the front door but by then the driver had closed that door and as he pulled away I saw his ugly laughing face in the tall side mirror.

"Grandma!" I yelled, and waved my arms around as I ran after the bus. I didn't see her face—just a puff of smoke coming out her window. In a moment they were gone and I had no idea where I was, so I just stood on the bench until I caught the next bus. The driver let me ride for free after I told him I'd lost all my money but he said he couldn't catch the other bus and so really I didn't know where I was going. I kept looking out the window for a clinic but after a long ride I spotted the bus stop where we first began in our neighborhood so I knew I had missed where Grandma was going. I pressed the STOP bar and got off. I waited and waited on the bench and I didn't have a watch but I knew it was a long time I waited because I stopped twenty-three buses and asked many of the same drivers if they had seen a grandma with a Chihuahua and an oxygen tank and all of them said they had not seen hide nor hair of her. I don't know what happened to the driver who tricked me. But I began to think that maybe Grandma drove him nuts and he had just pulled his bus over and quit.

So I ran around the field and threw rocks at signs, jammed sticks down ant hills, drew funny faces in the dirt, and did things until a bus pulled up and Grandma got off just about dragging her oxygen tank and clutching poor Pablo so hard he had fingerprints left on his sides like when I squeeze the loaves of white bread in the bakery. I got the buggy loaded back up and carted her home.

"You just won't learn," she kept saying. "That's your

problem in a nutshell. Everybody tries to fix you up but you. Maybe you can't be fixed," she continued. "Maybe you're one of those broken things that stays forever broken."

I just hung my head and felt bad again, like I had always felt bad with her when I had done something wrong and she really let me have it.

Finally I got smart enough to change the subject. "What'd the doctor tell you?" I asked.

"He said the smoking is definitely making me better," she said. "And that I'd be cured by now if I smoked a better brand."

So when we passed the convenience store I went in and bought her some good smokes with the last of my emergency money and that made her happy with me.

It was already dusk but from down the road I could see Dad's car in the driveway and as we got closer he was standing on the porch holding a beer in one hand while watching us through an old spyglass and tottering back and forth on his heels as if he were on the high seas.

I pulled up with Grandma and helped get her out of the buggy as he circled around us.

"I've been waiting all afternoon," he said, and pointed to a bandage over his arm muscle. "Got something special to show you."

He ripped the bandage off with a flourish. There

was a slick tattoo of my baseball jersey on his arm where the skull tattoo had been. When I reached out to touch it he got me in a headlock and rapped his knuckles on my bald spot and it hurt but it didn't bother me because I was grinning like a carved pumpkin with the light shining out my eyes and ears. I never thought anybody would tattoo my name on their arm.

"Were you drunk when you did it?" I asked.

The corners of his mouth curled up like warped paper.

"I was out *celebrating*," he replied with the curlicues winding and unwinding like a yo-yo. "Nobody gets a tattoo when they are sober! This one's not finished yet. After you win the championship I'll have your record—5 wins, 0 losses—tattooed along with 'PAL Champs.' "

"Did Leezy get one?" I asked.

He smiled. "Next time you see her, ask about her ankle," he suggested slyly.

"Can you move your arm?" I bleated. "Your BO is killing me."

He tightened his grip as I twisted my head like a cork. I tried to pull back but it felt like my neck was being snapped off. "I've been thinking again," he singsonged into my ear. "Since tomorrow is the big day we gotta pay our respects to my Humpty *buddy*."

"Who?" I croaked.

He dragged me across the porch and down the stairs as my legs and feet twisted behind.

"Let him go," Grandma barked out. "You're ripping his darned head off."

"I'm just horsing around," Dad said. "Don't get bent out of shape."

"Where are you going?" she asked.

"None of your business," he yelled over his shoulder as he dragged me to the car. "Get in," he ordered, opening the door and wrestling me onto the seat. He slammed the door, then walked around to his side.

"Don't wait up," he yelled to Grandma. "And whatever you do, don't cook. I don't have time to clean up after you later."

As soon as he sat down he reached into the back and pulled a can off a six-pack.

"Dad, you shouldn't drink and drive," I said, still catching my breath. "It scares me."

"Then you drive," he snapped back, and kicked open his door.

"That would scare me too," I said, and rolled my head around on my neck like I was trying to screw it down for a rough ride.

"Then don't worry about a beer," he replied, and pulled his door shut. "And another thing, don't get worked up over the small stuff in life, otherwise it will kill you." He started the engine and reversed quickly into the street. "Save your worries for the big stuff, like figuring out a plan for you to stay with me and Leezy. We got to get around your mom. You got any ideas on how to do that?"

I didn't. And I didn't want to "get around" Mom. I wanted to run straight at her and bury my head right in her middle and have her wrap her arms under me and hold me and sing sad country songs like she does so I could hear the sound of her voice nuzzling around inside her belly.

"Well, I got some ideas," Dad continued. "Possession is nine-tenths of the law, and right now," he said, reaching over to clamp his hand on my shoulder, "you and I are a team. Right, buddy?"

"You're my dad," I said.

"You're *my* kid," he replied, and gave me a shake.

"Can I turn on the radio?" I asked.

"No noise," he said. "We gotta be quiet."

I didn't talk and he didn't talk and I wished I was driving the car because it would give me something to do besides shift around in my seat and knead the flesh on my arms and legs as if I was made of Silly Putty and could stretch and press myself into a big dumb lump. After a while Dad turned off the headlights and we went down a dirt road until he pulled in between two weeping willow trees.

"This is the back door to Storybook Land," he whispered. "At night I call it Scary-Book Land." He came around to my side with the rest of the six-pack hanging from his wrist like a chunky bracelet.

"I love this place in the dark," he said, and gave me a boost up over the chain-link fence. He climbed up the side and swung himself over the top. "Follow me."

I felt like I was walking through the dark pages of a fairy-tale book that had been closed for the night and dropped by the side of the bed.

It *was* scary. Every time the trees moved I kept thinking the Giant was on the loose. When we passed the Old Lady's shoe house I thought only really crazy people would live inside a smelly shoe and I had a feeling her kids were running wild with nothing to do but come after me. I figured the Wolf was going to swallow me for good, the Crooked Man seemed really mean and was going to hit me with his stick, and when we finally arrived at Humpty Dumpty he looked like somebody whose big belly had crushed his skinny legs and was now hurt and crying because no one could ever help him get better. During the day all the stories seemed to teach lessons on how to be good and smart, but in the dark all the stories seemed to be about people with problems. Maybe that's why Dad liked them, I thought. He fit right in. And now I did too.

"I'm scared, Dad," I said.

"Don't be," he replied. "It's only make-believe."

"No, I mean about not living with Mom. I'm *scared* to tell her that."

"Well, I think you should," he said. "I think you should call her and tell her you're staying with me and let her hear it straight from the horse's mouth."

"No," I said. "She'll be upset."

"I'll take care of her," he said. "You just be Joey and tell her you want to live with your dad."

"Dad, I need to tell you something about me being me," I said.

"So tell me," he said. "I'm listening."

"Okay," I said, and I tried hard to get the first word of where to start but it just seemed impossible to do because the more I tried to start talking the more chopped up the ideas became. I wanted to tell him that I thought we were a lot alike and we were both hyper and needed medicine and we shouldn't live together since I wanted to live only with Mom, but that I loved him, yet liked living with her more and he shouldn't hate me for that but there didn't seem to be any way of saying so because, even though I knew how I felt, the words were all piled up against the door in my throat and when I tried to speak I couldn't and it made me sick that I felt less like me and more like something I was becoming but didn't know yet.

"Here's what I *think* you want to say," Dad said before I could speak. "A lot of changes are taking place all at once. What you have to do is just go with the flow and work through them. That's all. You'll see. Don't even try to talk about it. Just ride it out. Believe me, you and I are two of a kind, so I know what you're going through. Just relax."

"That's not it," I said. "No."

"Well, consider this," he said, and opened another beer. "You know one of the reasons why I am the way I am, Joey? Because my mind is constantly focused on perfection—on the way life ought to be—and I can imagine perfection in everything but I can't get perfection in real life. Not from me. Or your mom, or my mom, or Leezy. Which is why I need you to win tomorrow. All my life I've wanted to be a winner and you're the guy who can make that happen and be my little corner of perfection."

"I want to be perfect," I said. "I do."

"Then just take it easy. You don't have to pitch a *perfect* game. A win is all I want."

"I mean I've already made a mistake," I said. "I'm not perfect." And I wanted to tell him about how I should still be on my medicine, that it was a mistake to not have told Mom what I did. It was a mistake to think I could work it all out by myself. I just didn't want anyone to get upset with me, because all my life people had been upset with me. It was a mistake not to listen to Mom because she told me not to do things for her or for him, but for me. But I didn't listen to her and now it was too late to change things back and I was upset with myself.

"Nobody's perfect," Dad said. "You just have to be better than the other guy."

"Dad, I'm scared," I said. "Let's go back."

"Not yet," he said. "I saved the best for last. I know how to turn on the bumper cars."

That got me. "I love bumper cars!" I shouted.

"Me too," he said. "When I sneak in at night I turn them on and just go whizzing around the floor and bang into stuff by myself. Always better to hit than to be hit," he said.

Then before I could tell him that I always imagined him as a bumper car on the loose bouncing off everything up and down the streets and in and out of rooms, he jumped up and ran down a little path and I ran right behind him.

When we got to the bumper cars I saw one with a cross-eyed clown face painted on the front and I knew that was the one I wanted. Dad lit a match to see and opened an electric panel next to the operator's chair. He fiddled around for a few minutes until he flicked a switch and the cars jerked forward a bit.

"It's show time," he yelled. "Every man for himself."

I was already in my car when he hopped onto the hood of a car painted up like an Easter egg, and I knew I was going to turn him into a real Humpty Dumpty. I stepped on the pedal and when I looked up I saw sparks trailing down behind me where the power pole touched the ceiling, and I imagined my thoughts being pushed out like sparklers. I was smaller than him so my car was faster. About the second time around I got him in my sights and slammed his car into a corner. He tried to work his way into the middle of the track but I slammed him again and wedged him between two cars. I kept backing up and slamming into him, then backing up and slamming into him and his head was snapping back and forth like I was shaking him real good and finally he yelled, "Enough already!"

But it wasn't enough for me. I kept letting him have it. He stood up on his seat and tried to jump to another car and I hit him again and he lurched forward and there was a burst of sparks that showered down on us like a Fourth of July rocket blowing up in front of my eyes. Dad hollered out and all at once my car stopped moving.

"My hand!" he cried, and hopped around on the smooth metal floor. "I got hold of the electric pole and it zapped me. Well, at least it's not you," he said, blowing on his hand. "You have to pitch. All I have to do is yell. Good thing it didn't get my mouth." He began to laugh like some maniac character who eats flies for supper, and I began to laugh too, not because his hand was burned but because suddenly I seemed full of electricity and I imagined if I opened my eyes real wide and my mouth and nose and ears and you looked inside of me you'd see nothing but sparks flying around.

"Does it hurt real bad?" I finally asked.

"Nay," he said. "When I was a kid—and this is the God's honest truth—Granny used to give me a paper clip and tell me to put it in the wall socket because she knew a zap settled me down. Heck, even these days a couple a kilowatts now and again helps put me to sleep."

"Then give me five," I said, laughing.

"You're a sick puppy," he said. "I got a blister the size of a pancake on my hand and you want to slap it."

I just laughed even louder. "Splat!" I said, imagining the blister popping open as I smacked it.

"We better get out of here," Dad said.

We went back to the car. "Open one of those beers for me. It'll keep my bad hand cool while I drink."

I did as he told me and we drove back to the house.

"Well, tomorrow's the big game," Dad said. "Get a good night's sleep."

"Okay," I said. I was exhausted. But as I walked to my room I knew I wasn't going to sleep. I hadn't slept right in days. I was up so much even Pablo was growling at me for keeping him awake. I lay in bed and listened to every wheezing breath Grandma took and I rubbed the used patch on my belly like Aladdin rubbing his lamp and whispered, "I wish I was home with Mom. I wish the game was over. I wish I was normal again. I wish Dad didn't scare me. I wish . . ."

13

THE MOON

I was just getting a little too nervous at the breakfast table. I sat down and stood up. Down and up. Down and up.

"Make up your mind," Grandma said. "You gonna be jack-in-the-box? Or jack-out-of-the-box?"

"Can I get back to you on that?" I blurted out, and laughed and forgot why I was laughing and just felt hollow inside.

"You're nuts again," Grandma said, and she stood up and went to the bathroom.

As soon as she was out of sight I reached for the telephone. I punched in the numbers for home and it rang and rang and I started thinking that Mom wasn't at home or at work and I got it mixed up in my head that she had gone someplace and hadn't told me—like Mexico again although I knew she hadn't but maybe she had anyway. She probably went where life was a lot easier and where she'd be happier without me pestering her. Maybe she got tired of worrying about me. I figured if I started walking now, by the time I got home she wouldn't be there. Not even a note on the table. Nothing. And all her stuff would be packed and gone. I'd open her closets and they'd be empty except for the old things that reminded her of life with me and she'd have left them behind just like she was leaving me. And everything in her drawers would be gone. All her perfume and jewelry and shoes and magazines, and the only thing left in her room would be the blurry pictures of me in motion because she didn't want to be reminded of her old life now that she was busy making a new life. I was desperate to see her and have her hold me and even though a small part of me said I was thinking out of control, I was too far out of control to listen and as the telephone rang I suddenly remembered that Mom didn't have a license anymore and couldn't pick me up if I wanted her to so I said to myself, "Just walk home anyway, just go out the door and follow the road and it will get you home," and even though I felt my legs were full of springs and ready to walk around the planet I knew I wouldn't get there fast enough to stop her if she was running away. Then I thought of Dad's car so I hung up the phone and went into his room where he was still asleep and I knew he'd sleep for a while because there were so many empty beer bottles on the floor neatly lined up around his bed like a brown picket fence. I picked up his pants where he had folded them over a chair back and fished the keys out of the pocket and crept up the hall, when Grandma called to me from the bathroom.

"Get in here," she said, and I thought she had seen me take the keys and I was going to tell her I planned to wash the car but she only said, "I need your opinion on something."

I stuck my head around the corner and almost screamed, but I caught myself. Grandma had pulled half a cheek full of loose skin all the way back behind her jaw where she had it gathered in a wad and clipped to her ear with a clothespin. "Don't you think I'd look better with a face-lift?" she asked, and breathed through her mouth like a fish out of water. "I met someone nice at one of your ball games and he said I must have looked good twenty years ago."

I didn't know what to say but opened my mouth anyway and said, "You better watch out. If you pull the skin too tight it might rip apart like when you pull Play-Doh too hard."

"That's a nasty thought," she snapped, then looked into the mirror again and checked the color of her tongue, which was gray-looking and cracked like a dried-up bar of gas station soap. I didn't want to see anything more and when she asked me to take the little plastic tongue scraper and scrape the gray gunk off her tongue I just moaned as if I had seen a ghost and turned and ran down the hall.

I tugged Pablo out of the hole he had dug in the couch cushion and ran out the front door. I got into the car and moved the seat all the way forward like Dad had showed me. Then I took the key and stabbed it over and over at the little keyhole but the key kept sliding away until I got my face really close to the slot and slowly wiggled it in. Then I glanced up at the front door to make sure that nobody was looking before I turned the key and slouched down and pressed the gas and the engine started. I pulled the gearshift down to R and the car backed up and I went straight out the driveway and right away I knew I was in trouble because I couldn't see where I was going and steer and press the pedals all at once so I pressed the gas and lurched back then looked up over the seat and by then I was already out in the middle of the road and before I could hit the brake the car flattened the neighbor's mailbox and slid down into a little rain ditch and stopped. I was so scared I just turned the car off and grabbed the keys with one hand and Pablo with the other and ran back across the street and into the house where I pushed Pablo back into his hole and raced up the hall where I darted into Dad's room and put the keys back in his pants. One good thing about wrecking the car was that it knocked some sense into me and I no longer thought Mom was trying to leave me behind and as I sneaked down the hall Grandma was still looking into the mirror only now she had both sides of her face pulled back and held in place with circles of Scotch tape.

"Give me a hand," she gurgled, and held the roll of tape out, and I did what she said and circled it from around her chin to the back of her head and around and around like I was wrapping up the Egyptian mummy in a scary movie.

Later, after Dad woke up and screamed at the sight of Grandma with her face-lift because she scared him half to death and had made a mess in the bathroom, he spotted the car across the street. I thought I was going to be in big trouble, but he didn't say anything more to me than maybe he forgot to put the car in park and it must have rolled down the drive overnight, because he had done that before. While he went to call a tow truck to pull it back to our driveway I turned the television station to one of those exercise shows where people were doing all kinds of hopping around and sweating, and I just did what they did and tried to wear myself out. But then Dad saw me doing push-ups and he turned off the TV.

"I want you to sit down and rest," he said, and scooted the coffee table back into its place and smoothed the carpet marks out with the bottom of his shoe. "You got the biggest game of your life tonight and I don't want you wearing yourself out. Now what do you want for breakfast?"

"Nothing," I said. "I'm fine. Just fine." And I didn't know what else to do so I went into my room. I sat down on the corner of my bed with Pablo and put the little speakers into my ears and listened to the tape. I pulled out my trumpet and started to play along, which must not have sounded very good because Pablo hopped down and began scratching at the door to get out, but I didn't stop playing. I kept thinking to myself that the music is the glue that keeps me together and so I played as loudly as I could.

The next thing I knew Grandma burst into the room and pulled the trumpet out of my hands. "You gotta knock that racket off," she said in a tight voice that sounded like her jaw was broken because she had it all taped up.

"I'm just keeping busy," I said.

"Well, try to keep busy doing something more quiet," she suggested.

"Yeah," Carter yelled from the kitchen. "Like cleaning."

I hopped up and went to the bathroom and closed the door before Grandma could get there first. I was going to get the cleaning supplies out of the cabinet but then I saw Dad's foamy shaving cream on the counter and suddenly thought it was a great time to do something I had been wanting to try. The Tijuana Brass tape cover had a naked woman buried under a mountain of whipped cream and since I didn't have whipped cream I thought shaving cream would do. I took off all my clothes except for my underwear and began to shake the can and spray foam all over my body. I started with my legs and inched my way up bit by bit and by the time I sprayed a big swirly beehive of foam on top of my head I didn't look anything like the tape cover. Instead, I looked like the abominable snowman. I started making moaning noises and I was hoping Grandma would come and knock on the door because I remembered a scary movie where the abominable snowman met the mummy for a showdown.

"Grand—maaa!" I wailed. "Grand—maaa!"

"What's going on in there?" she asked, and pounded on the door. "Are you ill?"

"Grand—maaa!" I wailed again. "Open the door."

She pushed the door open and I lunged at her. "Arghhh," I growled.

Her mouth popped open so wide it snapped the tape around her jaw and she screamed until she lost her breath and had to lean against the wall. I dropped to my knees with laughter and when she finally recovered she said, "I don't know what's gonna kill me first—a heart attack or a lung attack." Then she started to laugh too.

It was funny until Dad came around the corner and saw the shaving cream mess all over the bathroom.

"What has got into you?" he barked. "You're goofing around and making a mess and all I ask is for you to rest before the game. Now get in the shower, then clean up the floor and get back to your room. You hear me, mister?"

"Yes, Dad," I said. "I was only having some fun."

"This is not a fun day," he snapped back. "This is a serious day. We've got a big game ahead of us—not a shaving contest! Now do you hear me?"

"Can I get back to you on that?" I replied.

He jerked forward like he was going to take a swipe at me but Grandma stepped between us. "Calm down, boys," she said. "Save it for the game."

Dad turned and marched back to the kitchen, where he loudly announced that he was going to clean the oven, "because someone made a potpie mess again!"

"That will be the third time he's cleaned it this month," Grandma whispered to me.

I took my shower and went back to my room. I got dressed in my baseball uniform and sat in a chair until I couldn't do that any longer, so I got out my duffel bag and I filled it with all my stuff. Then I dumped it out and packed it again. I got tired of that so I lifted up my shirt and got a pen and started to draw tattoos all over my body. I kept doing that until Dad poked his head into my room and told me it was time to eat a little something then head out to the ball field.

When we got into the car Dad had his speech all prepared. "We're going to play like pros. With dignity. No tape players, no dogs, no phone calls, no rolling the ball to the plate, no weird stuff. Just pure baseball played by the rules."

"Do the rules really say no dogs allowed on the mound?" I asked.

"Don't question me, Joey," Dad snapped. "I'm a little tense and I have no patience for your shenanigans. So just do what I tell you and nothing more. You got that?"

"Dad," I said. "I'm not having fun."

"Get used to it," he replied. "Life isn't fun when all day long you can't do anything but mess up."

I wanted to say something back but I had such a bad case of the jitters that I zippered my lips because I was sure if I spoke it would be messed up and Dad would get even more tense.

By the time we arrived the parking lot was jam-packed and the stands were full. The towers full of lights were so bright that when I looked up at them my eyes jerked over to one side like when you yank your hand back from touching something too hot. I looked over at the green grass and it seemed to cool my eyes down, as if dipping my hand in ice water.

"There he is," Leezy announced when she saw me coming, "the king of the hill." Then she gave me a hug. "I've been thinking about you all day. Hope your dad didn't make you wash the walls. When he's nervous he is a cleaning fool."

I smiled. "I just cleaned myself," I said.

"Joey!" someone called out. I looked up into the stands and it was Grandma. She held Pablo up. He was wearing his lucky belly sweater. "Good luck!" she yelled, then looked away to cough.

"Come on," Dad said, and steered me toward the mound. "We have business to complete."

I followed him out to the mound, where he turned and put his hand on my shoulder.

"Caveman," he whispered, "don't let me down. I hate losing. Just hate it. Guys like us—you know, guys who have had their hard times—want to be winners too. Some lucky people are born winners. But you and I have to go out there and earn it. You know what I mean, son?"

"I do," I said. And I did. I knew everything there was to know about learning how to be a winner the hard way. I knew it down into my toes. And now I was with my dad and he was saying things to me about wanting to be a winner that I always felt but had never said to anyone. And here we were, wanting to be winners together. I had him and he had me and we were so alike it was as if I had a giant twin. I didn't want to let him down and I was hoping and praying that I could just get through this one last game before I unraveled at the seams like a baseball that had been smacked around one too many times.

Dad fit the new ball into my hand. Then he rolled up his sleeve and pointed to his tattoo. "You're undefeated, let's keep it that way," he said. "This is a championship game. I want you to cover first, cover home, and catch pop-ups."

"I'll try," I said. "I'll give it my best." Then I pulled up my shirt and showed him the tattoos I had drawn on with a pen.

He was puzzled. "What are they?" he asked.

"Patches," I said, poking them. "They'll keep me calm."

He frowned. "The only thing you need is determination," he said. "Now hunker down and beat these guys."

The umpire stepped forward and brushed off the plate and the crowd began to roar. "Batter up," he called as he adjusted his chest protector and mask. Dad trotted toward the dugout and our catcher punched his fist into his glove.

"Come on, Pigza. Blow 'em away!" he hollered.

I looked at the catcher's mitt and nowhere else because I had the feeling if I started to look around my mind would wander off so I just threw as hard as I could and before long it was three up and three down.

Our team didn't score either and I was right back on the mound. I reared back and let one fly. But right away I could tell there was something wrong because I was trying to throw a strike and the ball went over the umpire's head. The catcher jumped up and threw it back to me. I gripped the ball and it felt like a jumping bean in my hand. I looked up at the full moon. It was big and round and solid. "Come on, Joey," I whispered. "Don't crack up." Then I looked back at the catcher. He smacked his glove.

"Put 'er right in here," he shouted. "Come on, Pigza."

I did and the batter hit it in the gap for a double. Right away Dad was yelling, "Lucky hit! Come on, Joey. Hunker down!"

"Focus," I said to myself as I circled around the mound. "Just take it easy and focus."

I listened but the ball didn't. I walked the next two batters and loaded the bases and Dad was hollering stuff from the side but I wouldn't even look at him.

On the next pitch I got lucky and the batter hit into a double play that drove in a run and the following batter hit a fly ball to the outfield.

When I returned to the dugout I pulled my hat down over my face and tried not to hear a thing—not Dad or Leezy or even Grandma and Pablo. Inside my head there was a hissing sound like someone had poked a hole in me and whatever control was left inside was leaking out.

"You're up, Joey," Dad hollered.

As I grabbed my bat Dad dropped down on one knee and put his hand on my shoulder. He looked me in the eyes. "I want you to stand real close to the plate. That might help with your hitting and if a ball happens to come at you, just turn your back on it."

"Won't that hurt?"

"Not for long. Just take one for the team," Dad said. "Now suck it up and let him plunk you."

"Batter up!" the ump called, and I ran over to the plate and got real close and lifted the bat up over my shoulders. The pitcher reared back and let it go and I thought it was coming for my head so I dropped down on the ground.

"Strike one," the ump hollered.

When I stood up I turned and looked at Dad. He gave me the thumbs-up.

I inched even closer to the plate and dug my feet into the dirt. The pitcher went into his windup and let the ball fly. I turned my face away and squeezed my eyes together and the ball slammed off my helmet. I went tumbling backward and rolled across the ground. The ump dashed over and put his hand on my shoulder. "You okay?" he asked, and he looked scared.

I looked up at him. The funny thing was that I think the hit on my head was good for me. It hurt so much I could hardly think of anything else except for Dad, who started to trot toward me, and when I saw him coming I jumped up and ran down the first-base line. "I'm okay!" I kept shouting to the ump. "I'm fine. Play ball!"

"Yeah, he's okay," I heard Dad say. "He's got a head like concrete."

The next batter was the right fielder. The pitcher must have been shaken up more than me because he threw one in there that the batter turned on and blasted out over the fence. I let out a cheer and skipped to second and turned and ran backward to third and was going to walk on my hands all the way to home but when I rounded third base Dad slapped me on the butt and growled, "Stop your clownin'." So I settled down and trotted to the plate. I stood there and when the right fielder touched home he said, "Way to take one for the team or we'd just be tied."

I smiled like a goon but when I walked back to the dugout Leezy made a big fuss over my head and started to rub it. I pulled away and when I looked over at Dad he winked at me and I smiled. The side of my head was sore but it didn't matter because we were ahead and all I had to do was hold the lead and we'd win.

Our next batter hit a ground ball out and I went back to the mound. I took a deep breath and looked up into the night. The moon looked like a shiny splat-mark in the sky. Then I reared back and threw the ball. It hit the batter on the shoulder before he could duck. As he trotted toward first I left the mound and ran over to meet him.

"I'm sorry," I said. "I didn't mean it."

"It's okay," he replied, rubbing his shoulder. "I'm fine."

"It was an accident," I said. Then I felt Dad's hand on my shoulder. He steered me back toward the mound.

"Don't *ever* say you are sorry," he insisted. "They hit you first."

"I think something is wrong with me," I said.

"Don't disappoint me, Joey. Don't be a Humpty Dumpty on me and crack up."

"I'm not Humpty Dumpty," I said, shuffling my feet. "I'm just me."

"Then suck it up. A real champion doesn't make excuses." And he stomped back to the dugout.

I threw another pitch and hit another batter.

"You're losing control!" Dad barked. "Get a grip!"

The coach on the other team started yelling that I was hitting batters on purpose and the ump came out to the mound.

"Are you okay?" he asked. "Did that hit on the head knock you silly?"

"It was nothing," I said. "I'm just a little nervous."

By then Dad came running up. "He's fine," he said to the ump.

"I'm talking to the boy," the ump said. "You go back to the coach's box."

The funny thing is that as I was falling apart I looked over at Dad walking away with his arms swinging over his head and I felt as though his problem was my fault and if I could pull it together and win the game then he would pull together too.

After the ump settled everyone down he returned to his spot behind the plate and yelled, "Now, play ball!"

I reared back and let it fly. The ball went on a line directly into the stands. A few people scattered.

"Don't make me come out to the mound again," Dad shouted, "or I'll change more than just pitchers! I'll change your whole attitude! Now throw strikes!"

The catcher tossed me another and I reared back and let it go. It must have popped a car window in the parking lot because I heard glass flying and then I saw Dad run toward me with his face all pinched with anger. I didn't wait to see what he would do. I dropped my glove and ran toward the outfield. I passed the second baseman, passed the right fielder, and climbed the chain-link fence. At the top of the fence I looked back over my shoulder. All the players were in their positions. They hadn't moved an inch except to turn their heads in my direction. I figured Dad would be right behind me, and he would have been except that Leezy was standing in front of him with her hands on his shoulders.

"Get back here and finish the mess you started, you retard!" he shouted, and pointed at me. "Get back here before I have to track you down!"

I couldn't hear what other mean things he was saying but in my mind his giant voice was growling, "Fe Fi Fo Fum! I smell the blood of a little one." I jumped down from the fence and rolled and stumbled through a rough field and when I reached the road I ran toward a cluster of lights.

14

THE MALL

By the time I got inside the mall there was only one thing on my mind. Call home. But I didn't have any money. So when no one was looking I ran up to the wishing well and began to scoop all the change out and put it into my hat. It didn't make me feel good to be stealing other kids' wishes, but then I thought there must be some nice kid out there who if he knew me would make a wish that I was home with my mom and wouldn't mind if I used his wish money in the pay phone to make it come true.

After I cleaned out the well I went into the grocery store and handed the cashier my hat full of change. "Can I have quarters for this?" I asked.

She shrugged. "Sure," she said, and began to count it out. It was mostly pennies and it took her forever.

Once I got the quarters I ran to the pay phone and

shoved them all in the slot and dialed the number. As soon as Mom answered I blurted out, "I have to tell you my *secret*."

"What, Joey? What's wrong?"

"I haven't been taking my medicine and I thought I was normal but I'm not and now I'm like my old self and I'm in trouble with Dad and I'm really scared."

"Slow down," she said. "Just take a deep breath and let's take this one step at a time. I thought you were pitching tonight?"

"I was, but then I lost it." And I told her as fast as I could what happened and the whole time I was looking left and right just expecting Dad to explode into the store and grab me.

"Joey, now listen to me," Mom said. "I'll have to borrow the car and then I'll come get you. It's going to take some time to do this so you have to wait for me. Where are you?"

"The North Side Mall," I said. "Where Steel City Sports is."

"Well, you wait out front for me," she said. "I'll be there as fast as I can, license or not. But you know how long the drive is, so it'll be a while. Okay?"

"Okay," I said. And when I hung up I ran outside to the front entrance and hid in one of those fancy hedges that spell out *Welcome* in cursive. I was all squatted down inside the *o* like a soldier in a foxhole. I peeked out at every car and person. I was so afraid to see Dad and I was so hoping to see Mom. A long time passed and then I saw her. A car drove by and parked under a light and when the door opened I saw a woman with red hair. I jumped out of my hole and started running across the asphalt. "It's me, it's me!" I yelled and waved my arms over my head, but as soon as I got close enough my heart stopped. Because it wasn't Mom. It was Leezy and there I was running toward her with no place to hide.

"Joey?" she said. "What are you doing here? Your father is looking for you everywhere."

"My mother's coming to get me," I said, hopping from one foot to the next. "You won't tell Dad, will you?"

"Not right away," she said. "Although he might be on his way to see me. So hurry into the store. You can hide from him in my office while we figure out what to do." She held both my hands tightly like they were the reins on a wild horse and we started to run.

"Did we win?" I asked.

"No," she said. "After you went AWOL they put Virgilio in and he couldn't hold the lead."

"Well, I didn't lose," I said. "When I left we were ahead."

"Technically," she said, "you took the loss. The bases were full when you left, and you were responsible for the runners."

"Oh," I said. "I thought Dad could still have a perfect record tattooed on his arm."

"Well, right now I feel like tattooing J-E-R-K on his forehead."

I smiled because I was a good speller.

"What happened to you on the mound?" she asked as we entered the mall and slowed down.

"I flipped," I said. "Dad flushed my medicine down the toilet and I became my old self and just went around the bend."

"I'll say," she said, agreeing. "Your dad's the same way. Right now he's gone off the deep end himself. He's got his ups and downs and I'm sure when he wakes up tomorrow he's going to hate himself for this—but I'm not going to make any excuses for him. He can tell you himself how he feels. Right now, what can I do to help?"

"I already called my mom," I said. "She's on her way from Lancaster."

Leezy looked at her watch. "I figure that's about three hours," she said. "Why don't you hang out in my office. I have a TV in there and you can watch it, and tell me what kind of car your mom has and I'll watch for her."

"Please don't tell Dad where I am," I said.

"I won't unless I have to," she said, and held me to her with her arms around my back. "We don't want him calling the police. But no matter, I'll see to it that he doesn't come here before your mom arrives. I know how to handle your father." She made a fist and nicked herself across the jaw. "You gotta fight fire with fire," she said.

I went into the office and for the next three hours I changed the channel about once every second. I wanted to watch everything and I couldn't get myself to watch any one thing so I just spun through the channels so fast that I nearly watched them all at once and that seemed to keep me in one spot.

Finally Leezy came in. "Joey," she said. "Your mom's out back. Come on."

I stood up and ran in the direction Leezy pointed. A door was open and I ran out onto a loading dock. Mom was standing in front of the car and I just ran off the edge of the dock and right into her arms and knocked her back against the fender.

"Easy, partner," she said as I slid down the front of her dress like a cartoon character who had run into a wall.

"You better get going," Leezy said. "I'm keeping Carter at bay, but you know how unpredictable he can be. And once you guys have gone I'll call and tell him what's happened."

"Thanks," Mom said.

I turned and waved to Leezy, then hopped up and

jumped into the passenger seat. Mom got in and we took off across the parking lot.

"There is a patch in my purse," she said. "It won't kick in for a few days, but the sooner we get you started the better."

I reached in and found it. I ripped open the package and slapped the patch on the back of my arm. She reached over and rubbed the side of my face and it was the best thing I ever felt.

"Who was that woman?" Mom asked.

"Dad's girlfriend," I said.

"She must be a saint," Mom remarked.

"She is," I said, and I was smiling because she was a saint for me.

"This visit with your dad has been a fiasco," Mom said, shaking her head.

"It's not your fault," I said. "I wanted to see him."

"And if I didn't let you see him I thought you'd always blame me for keeping you away. Now you know on your own," she said.

"But I wanted Dad to work out," I said quietly. "I wanted the whole family to be together."

"He blew it again," she said. "Looks like it's just you and me."

"Leezy said he'll hate himself in the morning," I said.

I could see in her face that she was going to say

something mean. Then she paused, and just looked tired.

"Yeah," she said. "That's one of his biggest problems. He always hates himself the next morning."

"He needs meds," I said.

"He's been self-medicated forever," she replied.

"He needs help," I said.

"He doesn't believe in help."

"He needs me," I said.

"Sure he does," she said. "But he's still too messed up to know it." And when she said that, the tears started running out of her eyes and her driving got all curvy.

I knew it was my turn to cheer her up. "One thing about Dad," I said, "is that he is a better driver than you are."

She started to laugh. "There is a Kleenex in the glove box," Mom said as we headed toward the highway. I pressed the button and the little door dropped open and hit me on the knee.

"Oh my god!" I shouted. "Pablo is with Grandma back at Dad's house!"

"Aw, sugar!" Mom hissed and hit the brakes. "Sugar, sugar, sugar! I knew this was too easy." We slowed down until we could turn around. "Okay," she said. "We'll get him."

"We have to," I said. "He's the rest of our family."

"Then he better start acting like he wants to stick

with us. That darn dog is destined to be forgotten. Next time get a bigger dog. This one's like, out of sight, out of mind, if you know what I mean."

I did. But I wasn't getting another dog. "That would be like me saying to you, next time pick a different kid."

"Well, we couldn't have that," she said, and pulled me over to her side. "Nope. I like the one I got right here."

I was the right kid. And she held me to her side until we pulled up to Dad's house.

"His car is here," Mom whispered. "He's probably waiting for us."

"Look," I said, pointing. "Pablo is tied to a leash out front." I hopped out of the car. I ran over to Pablo, who started yapping like I had come to strangle him instead of save him. My hands were shaking so hard I couldn't get the clip undone on the leash and he kept prancing from side to side and all I could think about was how I should put a patch on him. I looked up for a moment and saw Grandma pull the curtain to one side and glance out the window. Then she disappeared and I heard her unsnapping the locks on the door and figured Dad would be on me in a second. I pushed Pablo over to his side and pinned him down and got the snap opened and grabbed him and ran to Mom's car and as we tore down the road I glanced into the side mirror and there was only a tiny image of

Grandma standing on the sidewalk. She was waving and at first I thought she was telling me to come back, then I realized she was waving goodbye. I leaned out the window and yelled, "So long! I'll miss you!" I felt sorry for her because she was stuck there with him, and he wasn't nice. He *wasn't* like me only bigger, as Mom had said. He wasn't like me at all.

After a minute I looked over at Mom and said, "Do you think he'll ever really turn himself around?"

Mom's driving got all curvy again and she pulled the car over on the side of the road. "Family hug," she said, and put her arms around me and Pablo. She never could do two things at once, which was good, because when it came to hugging me I wanted her all to myself.